The Secret of
the Purple Lake

Yaba Badoe

Abuja London

First published in 2017 by Cassava Republic Press

Abuja – London

Copyright © Yaba Badoe 2017

A CIP catalogue record for this book is available from the National Library of Nigeria and the British Library.

ISBN (Nigeria) 978-978-55177-0-5
ISBN (UK) 978-1-911115-31-1
eISBN 978-1-911115-32-8

Printed and bound in Great Britain by Bell & Bain Ltd., Glasgow.

Dedication

For my godchildren - Ajani, Mukai, Joe, Ben, Allegra, Fynnie and Kaahiye - and the next generation of storytellers and readers - Issa, Emefa, Elorm and Lael - with all my love.

Contents

The Fisherman's Daughter   1

The Wild Princesses of Orkney   25

The Walrus Prince   45

Romilly The Golden Eagle   70

The Fish-man of the Purple Lake   96

1

The Fisherman's Daughter

A long time ago, during the days of the Ghana Empire, there lived a girl named Ajuba whose house was by the sea. Ajuba lived with her father, her mother and her brother, but it was her father she loved best of all. He was called 'the Man with Silver Nets' because every time he went out to sea, he returned with nets teeming with fish.

Early one morning, when Ajuba should have been helping her mother light the fire to cook breakfast, she followed her father to the seashore. 'Can't I come with you this time?' she pleaded, gazing up at her father. 'Please, Pa. I'll help you throw your nets into the ocean and if water comes into your boat I'll bail it out for you.'

'But who will help your mother if you come with me?'

Ajuba didn't know what to say. She didn't enjoy helping her mother clean and gut fish – not to mention the other household chores she avoided whenever she could: chores such as sweeping the yard and washing her brother's clothes.

'I'd rather be out at sea with you, Pa,' Ajuba mumbled. She was about to dawdle back home, when her father grabbed her hands and swung her round and round, making the sea and sky whirl around her.

'Would you like me to throw you to the fishes?' her father teased.

'Yes!' Ajuba screamed. 'Throw me into the sea and I'll swim alongside your boat and fill your nets with snappers.'

'One of these days I'm going to give in to you, my girl!'

Ajuba's father put her down on the ground. When she tried to stand up, she staggered from side to

side and toppled on to her bottom, like an old woman drunk on palm wine.

Before he set off, the Man with Silver Nets rubbed a special lotion of coconut oil on his skin, for protection against any danger he might encounter out at sea. The shark's tooth he wore around his neck for good luck shone and his skin glistened as he pushed the canoe into the water. He leapt into the boat, paddling on one side and then the other, until the only thing he could see was a speck on the shore waving at him: his daughter, Ajuba.

That evening, around dusk, when the heat of the day rested like a moist blanket on the sea, the village women helped the fishermen drag in their nets. Ajuba and her mother waited for her father. 'Perhaps he went out far this time,' her mother said, 'to find us deep-water fish.'

But twilight came and still there was no sign of the Man with Silver Nets. Ajuba and her mother huddled together, scanning the sea for his canoe. Apart from tiny crabs scuttling about their feet, and the sound of frogs croaking in the lagoon, everything was quiet.

At midnight, Ajuba's brother came out of the family house to join his mother and sister, for there was still no sign of the fisherman.

At daybreak, just as a breeze rustled the palm trees and the sea began to stir, three crows shattered the morning calm. They flew screaming through a coconut grove and circled the family hut. The birds perched on the roof, but then flapping their wings they leapt up and down, as if the roof was alight with flames.

The villagers ran out to see what was happening. Ajuba's mother flung coconut husks at the birds to keep them away from the hut. But they returned cawing, an omen of death in the family. It was then that one of the villagers pointed to the sea. There, on the milky horizon, was the fisherman's black canoe coming home with the tide. The canoe was empty.

***

Life changed in the village. The cocks stopped crowing, hens stopped laying eggs, and children sickened beneath the noonday sun. Then, one after the other, tethered goats disappeared and snakes, which had once only come out in the moonlight, flaunted themselves by day. Over seven months the village fishermen caught nothing but tiny fish, mangoes dropped green from trees, and children spat out fruit poisoned by maggots.

One evening a cloud of vultures dropped seeds over the village farmlands. The next day, giant thistles sprung up and choked the ripening corn. Everyone grew lean.

On the advice of the oldest man in the village, the community decided to seek help from Nana – an old woman who lived at the edge of the forest. Nana was as gnarled and thin as the trees that twisted around her hut, and her face was wrinkled like a tiger nut. She understood the ways of forest folk and could work their magic well. It was said that she could whistle dwarves down from trees and once, a long time ago, she had danced with leopards under a full moon.

A delegation, led by the old man, went to see Nana. After they described their troubles, she withdrew to sit beneath a Nim tree – the most ancient tree in her compound. Nana gently hummed to herself and when all around her was still, opened her cloudy eyes. 'Just as the forest claimed me,' she began in a low musical voice, 'so the sea must have its daughter.'

'What do you mean?' the old man asked.

'The child the sea wants,' Nana explained, 'is the daughter of the Man with Silver Nets. His spirit cannot rest until his bones are brought to land for burial. Only then will the village know peace and prosperity again.'

Ajuba's mother wept when the villagers came to take her child away. Ajuba clung to her mother screaming: 'I want to stay with Mame. I'll cook and clean. I'll do everything you ask me to do, won't I Mame?'

'This girl is my only daughter,' her mother cried. 'You can't take her. I forbid it!'

Deaf to their protests, the villagers prised Ajuba's fingers from her mother's waist. The woman dropped to the ground and, rubbing dust over her face, cursed the villagers for their wickedness.

The old man tried to soothe her by wiping her brow clean and assuring her that Kwame, greatest of all the gods, who created heaven and earth and everything on land and sea, would watch over Ajuba. But the woman cursed each and every one of the people who tore her daughter from her arms.

That night Ajuba was given one of Nana's potions to drink. She fell into a deep sleep in which she dreamed that hyenas carried her for miles along the seashore. When she awoke, she found herself alone on a strange beach. She would have cried had it not been for the reassuring sound of the sea calling her name.

The child replied by paddling along the shoreline and picking up brightly coloured shells. She was so absorbed in the purple, pink and gold shells that she didn't notice the sea changing. In a matter of seconds it receded a mile down the shore, then it yawned, turning into the mouth of a gigantic hippopotamus about to swallow the world.

Ajuba dropped the shells. She was about to scream when she heard Nana's voice telling her not to be frightened. But as the enormous wave curled around her and swallowed her deep down to its belly at the bottom of the sea, she yelled, terrified, convinced that she was tumbling to her death.

***

Ajuba's fall ended with a thud on the seabed. 'Have I become a ghost?' she asked.

She saw that her arms and legs were still the same and, to her astonishment, she could breathe under water. There wasn't much to see though, for the water hung gloomy and heavy like the sky on a stormy night. There weren't any fishes swimming about and there was no foliage, just dark waves rolling along an endless desert of sand.

'Where should I go from here,' Ajuba wondered. 'How am I to find my way home again?'

From out of nowhere a voice answered her question. It was the reassuring sound of Nana speaking: 'Ajuba, you are here to find your dead father's bones and return them to land for burial.'

'How am I going to do that? Can't you just let me go home again? My mother worries about me . . .'

'Listen to what I have to tell you, my child,' Nana replied sternly. 'To find your father, you must accomplish three tasks . . .'

'But I want to go home!'

'Didn't you want to follow your father out to sea?'

'That was different.'

'Maybe it was,' said Nana, 'but since you're here, if you want to survive what's in store for you, you'd better do what I say. Are you listening?'

Ajuba nodded, but before Nana could continue, she said, 'When I've done what's asked of me, will I get to go home again?'

'Stop asking questions and listen! First, you must steal a carbuncle, a sign of wisdom, from a whale and bury it in the Purple Lake. But be careful, for beside the lake lives a Fish-man who guards it with his life.'

'But where can I find a whale?'

'Follow the warm currents north,' Nana's voice replied. 'And there, beside a green island, you will see many whales.'

Eager to return home to her mother, Ajuba set off at once. She swam upwards to a part of the sea where fishes swim and food grows. There, she followed a group of brightly coloured fish looking for tepid water to play in. They soon stumbled into a flurry of warm waves that swept Ajuba northwards. Ajuba followed the warm current and then, after days of the sea being pitch black, Nana's voice came to her with the words: 'You've reached your destination, my child. Look around.'

Ajuba surfaced to look for the green island. She immediately dived back into the water, coming back up again when she'd plucked up the courage to face the biting wind. It was as cold as the blade of a new cutlass touching her cheeks.

To her left, Ajuba noticed an island covered with snowy peaks and black granite cliffs. There didn't seem to be anything green about the island yet, to her right, she noticed seven black monsters splashing in the sea.

'Whales!' Ajuba gasped. She looked closer and saw that the largest whale had whiskery growths over his body. 'Carbuncles!' she decided and swung into action.

Ajuba swam as close as she could to the biggest whale and then heaved herself on to its back. Its skin was as dark as her own, but a thousand times more slippery. Ajuba took a step forward and slid. She slithered this way and that, tumbling down mounds of black blubber, before colliding into the carbuncle on the whale's nose.

'What is that irritating tickle?' the whale rumbled as Ajuba landed on its carbuncle. The whale twitched its nose in an attempt to stop whatever was tickling it, but by now, Ajuba was clutching the whiskery carbuncle between its eyes. The whale stared at Ajuba in cross-eyed bewilderment. Although his carbuncle was exceedingly large, he was not, in fact, the cleverest of whales.

'What in heaven's name is that thing hanging on my carbuncle?' he bellowed.

He dived to the bottom of the ocean, while Ajuba hung on with all her strength. The whale resurfaced, spurting out a jet of water, but Ajuba clung on as determined as a soldier ant in battle. She tugged and heaved, shoved and pulled, until little by little she began to ease the growth from the whale's nose.

'My carbuncle!' the whale moaned. 'I've been working on it for years. It's the best in all of the seven seas and it's mine. It's *mine!*' He plunged into the water once again.

Unfortunately for him, Ajuba had already uprooted his precious possession and strapped it on to her back. When he lunged into the sea, Ajuba rolled off the whale's nose.

The weight of the carbuncle on her back thrust her under water. She would have sunk right to the bottom if she hadn't landed on the back of a smiling whale, a baby whale, who had been watching Ajuba's antics on its grandfather's back.

'Why are you stealing Grandfather's carbuncle?' the small whale asked, thumping her stumpy tail in the sea.

'I have to throw a carbuncle in the Purple Lake before I can find my father's bones,' Ajuba explained. 'You see, his bones have to be buried on dry land before my village can prosper again. Then, if all goes well, I'll be able to sleep on my own mat once more.'

'Oh, I see,' said the small whale, though she didn't really understand what Ajuba was saying and couldn't work out what a creature without fins, nor much blubber, was doing so far away from land. 'Would you like me to help you?'

'Will you help me? Will you *really* help me?'

'I wouldn't have offered if I didn't mean it,' the whale sniffed.

'In that case,' Ajuba replied, 'I'd really appreciate a ride to the Purple Lake.'

And so, together, they sped off to the Purple Lake.

They swam down south to where porpoises and dolphins play in the sun. They sped past islands with palm trees that catch shooting stars at night. And once, as they rested in the Caribbean, they saw the sea leap with hundreds of flying fish. Eventually, Ajuba and the whale found the Purple Lake hidden underwater at the bottom of a blue mountain range between two brooding volcanoes. The lake was still but restless, a dog snapping its teeth while asleep.

Ajuba and the whale approached cautiously. 'I must beware of the Fish-man,' Ajuba reminded herself.

While the whale hovered over the Lake, Ajuba
unstrapped the carbuncle from her back and flung
it down. As it hit the water, the Lake seethed and
snarled. Foaming at its centre, it rose up in the
form of a long, unfurling snake.

'Welcome to the Purple Lake,' the snake hissed,
swaying from side to side. 'I understand that you
have been sent here to find a path to where your
father, the Man with Silver Nets, lies swallowed by
the sea. I'm here to tell you, Ajuba,' said the snake,
'that if you want to find your father, you must go
to the Pink and Grey Cave, and teach the octopus
who lives there how to dance. Listen to the octopus while she dances, because she will tell you the
secret of how to succeed in your final task.'

Ajuba watched, mesmerised by the snake twisting
before her. She was so fascinated by what it was
doing that she didn't notice the *thing* creeping up
behind her: the Fish-man, a beast with the legs and
arms of a man, but the trunk and head of a fish.
In his hand he wielded an enormous sword made
from a thousand pointed shark's teeth. He swung
the sword over Ajuba's head, preparing to slice her
in half and then dice her up into pieces.

'Look out!' yelped the whale as she swatted the
Fish-man with her tail.

'Come on,' Ajuba screamed. 'Let's get out of here!'

Ajuba leapt on to the whale's back. She glanced over her shoulder and saw the Fish-man running towards her, waving his sword of shark's teeth above his head. But the whale was moving faster than he was, and so, quicker than lightning, the pair fled the Purple Lake, leaving a cloud of sand behind them.

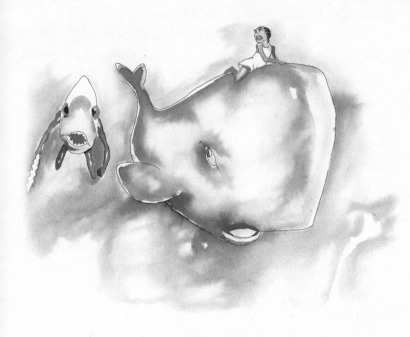

***

Now, the path to the Pink and Grey Cave is covered with scuttling crabs and spiky black sea anemones. Red and blue jellyfish hang in the water like lights suspended by invisible threads. Ajuba and the whale followed the lights towards the cave, carefully avoiding shelves of jagged coral. The whale breathed in to squeeze past them, and Ajuba ducked to avoid hitting sea bats that squawked when she touched them. The entrance to the cave was terrifying. It gaped, dark and mysterious; a passageway to another world.

'Would you please wait for me here, Whale?' Ajuba said to her companion. 'And if I'm not out soon, come and fetch me. OK?'

Ajuba drifted into the silence. A current lifted her up to a space shining with light: the Pink and Grey Cave. The light gave off a mysterious glow that made Ajuba feel as if she were floating in a dream.

The further up Ajuba floated, the brighter the mother-of-pearl shone. At first the light dazzled her, but gradually she made out a creature with eight legs drifting towards her from the centre of the cave. 'That must be the octopus that I have to dance with,' Ajuba decided.

As the creature sashayed towards her, Ajuba was struck by the clearness of its skin. It appeared transparent, for the light from its mother-of-pearl surroundings shone right through it, giving it a radiant, otherworldly sheen.

'Shall we dance?' Ajuba asked the octopus, as it arrived in front of her.

'Dance?' answered the octopus. 'Dance?'

'Come now. Let me show you.' Ajuba took a tentacle in each of her hands and began to stamp her feet and shake her hips the way she danced with her friends during village festivals. Under water, however, instead of drummers beating out a rhythm, there were crabs tapping their claws against conch shells, and the whale thumping her tail against the cave entrance. Ajuba stomped across the cave, making waves with her shaking body. The octopus copied her movements, transforming its tentacles into the arms of a belly dancer. While the creature danced it sang a song, which Ajuba listened to carefully.

'A fish sleeping on a full belly is safer than a hungry fish,' the octopus sang.

Eager to make sense of the song, Ajuba repeated the words – unaware that the creature was coiling a tentacle around her waist, another around her neck. Then, like it always did when it wrapped itself around something tasty, the octopus started squeezing.

'Stop!' Ajuba yelled. 'You're hurting me.'

The octopus kept on doing what it did instinctively. It hugged Ajuba so tightly, in fact, that struggling to breathe, she spluttered. Just as she was about to faint, the whale heard her cries for help and thundered into the cave. The small whale took in a deep gulp of water, spat it out and blew the octopus right across the cave. It crumpled in a heap of tentacles on the floor.

'Are you OK?' the whale asked Ajuba.

Ajuba touched the whale gratefully. 'Thanks to you, I've done it,' she said. 'Who would have thought it? I've taught an octopus how to dance!'

'You've done well, my child,' a faraway voice confirmed. 'You've done very well indeed. Now your next task is to find a tiger shark in the turquoise Sea of Cortez and ride it, because only a tiger shark can take you to your father's bones.

Ajuba and the whale looked at each other in horror. Tiger sharks are among the most ferocious fish in the ocean. What is more, the Sea of Cortez is where pirates and mutineers used to sail in search of treasure. It is said that sometimes, on stormy

nights, the ghosts of cargo boats can be heard crashing against rocks amid the screams of drowning sailors.

***

Ajuba and the whale trembled as they approached the turquoise sea, fearful of haunted galleons and petrified of tiger sharks. Even though the water was warm, goose pimples dimpled Ajuba's skin.

'I have to ride a tiger shark,' she kept saying to the whale, to pluck up courage. 'I have to ride a tiger shark, if I want to find my father's bones and return home to my mother.'

Ajuba repeated the words a third, and then a fourth time. The whale knew that her friend without fins and blubber was desperately trying to reassure herself, so to keep the girl's spirits up, she swam along calmly.

It isn't hard to find tiger sharks in the Sea of Cortez. They prowl about in packs of seven, howling at the sun. Their cries are carried by the wind for miles, warning fish and men that danger is close at hand. Ajuba heard the baying of sharks, followed by the snapping of teeth as one of them caught a large kingfish. When she heard the sound of the shark wolfing down its meal, she recalled the words of the octopus: 'A fish sleeping on a full belly is safer than a hungry fish.'

'Let's head towards that one,' said Ajuba, nudging the whale in the direction of the shark gobbling down food. 'It's just eaten, so it may be less fierce than the others.'

The whale agreed. They swam up quietly behind the shark, which by this time was so satisfied with his large meal that he had left his friends to take an afternoon nap. Indeed, by the time Ajuba and the whale had reached him, his eyes were closed.

Ajuba carefully climbed behind the shark's dorsal fin. The fish continued snoozing, dreaming of a feast of prawns and shrimps, laced with a brace of red snappers. He yawned, unaware of Ajuba on his back.

'Well, ride him then,' the whale whispered. 'You've got to ride him, you know.'

Ajuba shut her eyes. Then, with an almighty kick, she hit the tiger shark. The shark growled, angry at being woken up. He roared, looking from left to right, in case he could eat whatever had disturbed him. He couldn't see Ajuba, but he could feel something on his back: something that was clutching on to his fin and hugging his sides.

The shark shook himself to see if the thing would fall off. It didn't. He tried to snap behind his head, but couldn't reach far enough. He twisted in the water and somersaulted, but still Ajuba clung on.

Finally, impatient to rid himself of this burden, he charged into open water.

The shark moved with the speed of a giant canoe rowed by a hundred men. He thrashed water aside, beating his tail this way and that, lunging downwards, leaping towards the sky. Then, with an angry scream, he plunged down again. Ajuba hung on, even though her legs against the shark's razor sharp fin were frozen with terror.

Without realising where he was heading, the enraged tiger shark sped towards the whirlpool of Cortez. The currents there sucked him to the centre, to a place where his massive strength was as useless as a limp strand of seaweed. He spun round and around, whirling and turning, until he was moving so fast that he dissolved in a mass of red liquid. Ajuba tumbled down behind him, spiralling towards the centre of the sea.

As the currents sucked her down, they whipped her legs together – lashing them as if with rope. Ajuba spun around and as she did so, she changed. Her hair grew long, stretched by torrents of water; her body became taller and when she looked down at her toes, she saw they had turned into black fins. What's more, her legs had merged into a mermaid's tail, studded with scales that glistened like purple amethysts.

Ajuba was astonished at how the sea had transformed her. She was no longer a village girl but a Mami-Wata, one of the sea goddesses that people in her village whispered about on still afternoons when the sea rose angrily.

'Mame will never recognise me now,' Ajuba thought sadly, as she swished her new tail around. It sparkled in the water, so she twirled it again, turning her head to admire herself. As she looked, her eye caught a glimpse of something white glinting beneath her. She swam down to see what it was.

At the bottom of the whirlpool, stretching for miles and miles, was a graveyard. Shipwrecked vessels lay broken in pieces, their treasure tossed on the sand. Canoes, which had collided with giant fishes, lay ripped in two, their cargo of pearls scattered; and everywhere, for as far as Ajuba could see, were the skeletons of sailors and fishermen, their bones washed clean by sea dew.

'This is where my father must be,' Ajuba decided, swimming over the graveyard. She picked her way carefully through the skeletons. Some still had their swords strapped to them. Others had gold teeth or wore necklaces and bracelets. In broken cradles, she saw the tiny bones of sea-tossed babies.

Eventually, Ajuba found the bones she was looking for. She recognised the gold shark's tooth chain around the neck. Ajuba dragged her father's bones to a rock that stood far from any living thing. There, she lay down beside what was left of her father and wept. She cried for the games they had played together, the stories he had told her of windswept days out at sea and stars that fly at night. She cried for their round house by the seashore, and those warm dark nights when, half asleep, she would hear the murmur of her parents talking. Then, she cried for her mother who was cleaning and selling fish on her own, and the bed of matting that she would never be able to sleep on again. Ajuba wept, until the rock she was lying beside absorbed all her grief and rose up into a tall, grey mountain.

It was then that Ajuba heard the familiar thump of the whale's tail in water. 'My, how you've grown,' the whale exclaimed. 'You're almost as tall as I am now.'

'Am I?' Ajuba turned around, so the whale could take her in completely. 'I'm surprised that you recognised me with my new tail and everything. Do you like it?'

'Of course!' the whale replied. 'You look a bit more like us than those who walk on land. I reckon you've got the best of both worlds now.'

Ajuba grinned at her friend. Then she looked at her father's bones and wondered what to do with them. 'I suppose I'd better gather them up and return them to my village, hadn't I?'

The whale nodded.

Ajuba broke her father's bones one by one, before tying them in a bundle with a strand of her long black hair. In the middle of the bundle she placed her father's gold chain and shark's tooth, as proof that the bones belonged to the Man with Silver Nets. Then she strapped the parcel around her waist and, beckoning to the whale, they swam off to find the Gulf of Guinea off the west coast of Africa.

***

As they drew close to the beach where Ajuba's house stood, the friends hid themselves in the sea's shadow, in case the villagers saw them and were frightened. Ajuba swam in dark pools and sheltered behind rocks. Even so, a fisherman almost glimpsed her but she ducked in time. All he could see was a huge purple fin plunging under water. The man was her brother.

Early the next morning, Ajuba swam towards the shore. The round, firm house that she had lived in was still standing and her brother was patiently mending nets that had once belonged to their father. Seated beside him, Ajuba saw a woman feeding a child. A few yards away her mother sat on a stool, singing as she washed clothes. The wind carried her song over a coconut grove and swept it out to sea.

Ajuba whispered a message through the wind and suddenly, alert to her daughter's presence, the fisherman's widow left her washing to walk on the beach.

Scanning the waves, the woman called out, perturbed: 'Let me see your face, my daughter. Let me see you one last time, so that I can sleep in the knowledge that you are safe and well.'

Ajuba swam closer to the shore, but still kept her face hidden.

In desperation her mother stepped into the sea. Ajuba shrank back, in case the woman who'd suckled her and taught her to talk, the woman who'd tried to show her how to wash clothes and clean fish, and who she had clung to when the villagers had wrenched her away, should find her appearance upsetting.

'Daughter,' her mother cried, a sob in her voice. 'I dreamed of you last night, but when I touched you I didn't know if you were dead or alive.'

The fisherman's widow brushed tears off her cheeks. 'If you can hear me, Ajuba, please let me see your face. Then I'll know you've done what was asked of you, and our village will prosper. Let me see you, child.'

Her curly, black hair sparkling with sea dew, Ajuba slowly rose from the sea, strings of seaweed and shells around her neck.

The fisherman's widow stepped back in alarm, amazed at how tall her daughter had grown and how beautiful she had become. When at last she found her voice, she said, 'You are just as you were in my dream. You have become a daughter of the sea, Ajuba. But remember, before the sea claimed you, you were my daughter first.'

'I know, Mame!' Ajuba replied, blowing a kiss to her mother. 'I was your daughter first and I love you!' Ajuba removed the bundle of bones from her waist and threw it on to the beach where she'd once played.

'May the gods watch over you, my child! And may they grant you the grace to remember me as fondly as I remember you.'

'Goodbye,' Ajuba cried as her mother looked at her and waved from the shore.

'Goodbye,' the waves echoed.

Out at sea, Ajuba gazed at her home for a long time. She stared until the whale tickled her playfully and said, 'Come on, Ajuba. Let's go and find another adventure.'

And together they dived into the deep blue ocean.

2
The Wild Princesses
of Orkney

This is a story of long ago: when dragons lived in caves and frogs turned into Princes; when eagles hatched Princesses and mermaids swam beyond the coast of Scotland. All those years ago, there lived on the island of Rousay a King whose people wanted an heir. The King had three children already, three daughters named Jezebel, Delilah and Jael. But the King and his chieftains wanted a son to continue the ancient traditions of Orkney, the hunting of wild boar through Quandale forest in spring, and the supervision of trips abroad to pillage and plunder once the harvest was in.

After his third daughter, dark-haired Jael, was born, the King went to seek advice on how to get a son from Nancy of Hullion – a wise woman who lived alone with a cat in a tumble-down croft.

'What can I do for you, my Lord?' Nancy asked when she saw the King. Handing him a tot of

whisky, she saw anxiety pucker his brow. 'It'll be a son you're after my Lord, eh?'

The King nodded sadly. 'What can I do to have a fine healthy boy?'

'Are you sweet and tender to your lady wife?'

The King fell silent. It was well known on the island that, with the birth of each of his daughters, he had grown irritable and vexatious with his wife. He believed that their lack of a son was her fault and not his as well.

'If you can't be kind to her,' said Nancy, 'the next best thing to do is to follow an eastern practice. In those countries, my Lord, whenever girls are born and a boy is wanted, the last girl is reared as a lad. And in nine cases out of ten, the next child will be male.'

'So Jael must be like a son to me,' said the King.

'That's right,' Nancy replied. 'But it would help if you were kind to the Queen as well.'

From that day onward, little Jael's life changed. Her pink baby gowns were removed and she was given the blue silk ones the Queen had made for her long-awaited son. When Jael was a toddler, old enough for skirts, she was made to wear boy's britches. As soon as her thick curly hair began growing, it was cropped short – so that unless you knew her story, you would think on meeting her that she was a beautiful black-haired boy.

***

After the Queen's disappearance, the King tried to reform. He was aware that his treatment of the Queen and his subjects had been selfish, and he knew that he was to blame for the unhappiness on Orkney. He mourned the days of his youth, when the Queen's laughter rang through Trumland Castle and her smile had been like the first breath of spring after a dark Orcadian winter.

'It will never happen again,' he swore. 'I shall never abdicate my responsibilities. To make sure, I'll never marry again. Orkney must look for an heir elsewhere.'

The King's plan was to arrange for one of his daughters' husbands to become the next King of Orkney. That is, if and when they married. I say that because, though the Princesses were beautiful, their unusual upbringing both before and after their mother's disappearance had made them unconventional.

Even though Jael was still treated like a favourite son, wearing boy's clothes and her hair cropped, she was extraordinarily good friends with her sisters Jezebel and Delilah. All three of them spent as much time as possible out of doors. They rode to the forest for picnics of cheese and barley wine, and Jael taught her sisters the songs she had picked up on her outings with the King's men. She showed her sisters how to ride astride, instead of side-saddle as the ladies did in those days, so that they too could pursue foxes, deer and wild boar at royal hunts.

At the height of midsummer, during the simmer dim, when the sun never set and arctic seals splashed close to the shore, the three sisters walked along the jagged cliffs of Scabra Head and sang songs to the mermaids there. And during autumn, when the sun slipped away to the other side of the world and left Orkney dark and gloomy over winter, they picked blackberries at Westray – smearing their bodies with black juice till they looked like zebras dancing in moonlight.

'You'll never find husbands if you go on at this rate,' their old nursemaid, Betsy, scolded when they returned to the castle after one of their midnight jaunts. 'Staring at the stars indeed! You'll be calling yourself the three witches of Orkney next. You should be in bed, fast asleep, like your sister Jewel.'

The King's youngest daughter was quite different from her sisters. Jewel had her mother's golden hair and, like the Queen, was as patient as an old snail determined to reach its destination at the end of a long walled garden where seedlings are ripe for eating. But the journey Jewel was making was towards marriage and a hearth of her own.

Unlike her sisters, who frightened men with their bold glittering eyes, Jewel was gifted at reading men's hearts and making them fond of her. She spent hours chatting sweetly to the young

men of the court, while she sat embroidering a tapestry beside the fire in the Great Hall. And when winter evenings seemed tiresome, she fetched her mother's lute and sang songs of lands where the sun shines continuously.

'You're the jewel of my weary old heart,' the King said, smiling fondly at his daughter. But everybody knew that the real jewel of his heart was dark-haired Jael, who rode with her older sisters and laughed like the leader of a pack of howling wolves.

It happened that there was a man in the King's court who was particularly fond of Jewel. His name was Magnus. He was the son of the wisest and rowdiest of the King's chieftains – Lord Blackhamar of Blackhamar Lodge to the north-east of Rousay. Magnus had a strong but gentle face, a character at once manly and sensitive, and legs so shapely that even nursing mothers swooned at the sight of them.

Jewel received Magnus's attentions coyly, giggling at the fuchsias he picked her and the presents he gave her of shells and stones that he found along the shore. Jewel saw that Magnus was a kind man and, knowing that he was a well-placed son of Orkney from a family with a large estate, she fell in love with him.

As was the custom in those days, Lord Blackhamar went to the King to ask if Magnus could marry Jewel.

'Nothing would please me more,' the King replied, delighted at the thought of such a worthy son-in-law. 'But according to royal protocol, Jewel's elder sisters must marry before she can. Please tell Magnus to be patient. I'll try and get those strong-headed daughters of mine married off as soon as I can.'

***

A general call was sent through out the Norselands, and territories to the north and south, that the King of Orkney was looking for suitors for his three eldest daughters. Word had it that they were as sweet as Orcadian mead, as strong as Scottish whisky and as graceful as the seals splashing around Rousay.

'Just wait till they see your tempers,' laughed Betsy, scrubbing the long white backs of the three Princesses.

They cursed her roundly. 'We don't want to marry,' they yelled. 'Let sweet-tempered Jewel do our marrying for us. We won't make Princes out of frogs, will we sisters?'

But though they stormed and raged around Trumland Castle, and prowled in front of the fire like angry panthers, in their hearts they were secretly pleased at all the attention they were getting. That is, Delilah and Jezebel were pleased, but not Jael.

For the first time in her life she was told not to wear men's clothes. She was no longer allowed to go drinking with the young men at court, and was prevented from cutting her hair. At first she tore her dresses off and pounded at the King's door when Betsy told her that it was on his instructions that her clothes had been burnt.

'Father,' she cried, tears rolling down her cheeks. 'Am I no longer your girl-son, your favourite dark-haired Jael?'

The King hardened his heart, believing that what he was doing was in his daughter's best interest. 'You'll always be my Jael,' he replied, safe behind a locked door. 'But you've got to marry. You've got to marry so that Orkney can have a son and heir.'

Jael walked away from her father's door, disheartened, and resumed her wanderings across the moorland at the cliff at Scabra Head wearing a red velvet dress. She watched lights falling over the island of Eynhallow, and gasped when a clear sky revealed a night dazzling in star-brightness.

As Jael's hair grew, suitors came for her sisters. Jezebel, the King's eldest daughter, was the first to be put on show. She discovered, shut inside her room at Trumland Castle, that she had a flair for decorating herself. She daubed paint on her lips and eyes – one day spotted like a leopard, another striped angry like a tiger. Every day she met her suitors in the likeness of a new animal – red like a fox, purple in raven's feathers, or silvery-grey with eyes innocent as a seal. Her suitors were stunned by her gaudy beauty, her red fingers flashing through her hair, her lips hard and dark as rubies.

Princes from as far as the Orient came to court Jezebel. They brought her jewels and sweetmeats, rare exotic animals and servants to do with as she pleased. But Jezebel was interested in none of them. She pouted, stamping her foot angrily whenever they tried to make her smile.

'Do you think I'm a child?' she scowled. 'If you're the man for me, I'm not my father's daughter!'

One day a Cherokee Indian arrived on Rousay with a troupe of dancing bears and girls juggling golden balls. The man was tall with bright feathers pinned in his hair, and a face painted silver like an arctic fox.

As soon as she saw him, Jezebel knew she had found her man. She smiled at the tales he told of his people across the Atlantic: about how they hunted buffalo, grew maize and ate succulent fruits. She smiled as he told her about the Great Spirit he worshipped who had brought him safely to her castle and would return them home again. Taking him by the arm, Jezebel stepped into the prince's magic canoe and waved goodbye to Orkney forever.

By the time Jael's hair was curling beneath her chin, suitors were beginning to arrive for Delilah. Delilah locked herself in her bedroom, refusing to come out until she had arranged her hair. She patted and sprayed her auburn curls for hours, deigning to see her suitors only when she was bored and wanted someone to admire her.

One day she came to the Great Hall with her hair falling plainly down her back. The next day she plaited it elaborately with pearls laced between the braids. Every day she walked past rows and rows of men, turning them away despite the honeyed phrases they courted her with and the luxury they promised her.

'I'm not a fool,' she snarled, shaking her hair wildly. 'If you're the man for me, I'm not my father's daughter.'

On the longest day of the year, a Sikh Prince from India arrived on Rousay. His head was wrapped in a fat orange turban and, to keep out the Orcadian wind, he was swathed in a thick cashmere rug. When Delilah saw him, she suspected that he might be her man.

'What do you have under your turban?' she asked, tugging at her hair.

The Prince slowly unravelled his turban, revealing a long strand of thick black hair that touched his feet. Delilah stroked it lovingly, holding it to her cheek to feel its softness. Then, the Prince fondled Delilah's braids, and unravelled them to pass an ivory comb through her curls.

The Princess sighed with pleasure. Taking the Sikh Prince by the hand, she stepped on to his magic rug and waved goodbye to Orkney forever.

Now it was Jael's turn to marry. Her black hair had reached her shoulders and everyone wanted her to choose a husband. Magnus, Jewel's fiancé, was growing impatient – kind and worthy though he was.

'Haven't you seen anybody you like yet?' he asked Jael at the end of every week, after hordes of disappointed men had been sent off the island. 'There must be one of them, at least, that pleased you,' he scolded. 'Surely one of them would have done?'

'Quite right,' agreed the King.

'Do you want me to leave you, Father?' Jael asked.

'No, dear,' he replied, avoiding his daughter's eyes. 'It's just that a girl must marry.'

Jael blushed. She found choosing a man an awkward business. She much preferred her nightly walks around Rousay staring at the stars, and her daily visits to Nancy of Hullion for advice on how to grow herbs. 'Nancy of Hullion isn't married,' she mumbled.

'What's that you said?' shouted the King. In his old age he was becoming deaf.

'Oh, never mind,' said Jael. And shaking her hair loose, she took her hunting dogs for a walk on Scaqouy Head.

The next day, Jael decided to get the whole un-
pleasant business of marriage over by accepting
the first suitor she saw. It happened that the first
man to approach her that day was Leopold, a prince
of the Norselands. He had been living at the castle for over a year, trying to win Jael's heart. Leo,
as he was known to his friends, was a steady man
with a heart as big as a bear.

'Very well, I'll marry you,' Jael said petulantly, 'if
you make me a wedding dress from the feathers
of puffins.'

'I'll do anything you want,' Leo replied, staring at
Jael with soulful blue eyes.

Leo leapt into a boat to journey to the island of
Wyre. In those days there was a large colony of
puffins there, from which Leo hoped to pluck white
feathers for Jael's wedding dress. Had Leo had
more patience, he would have waited for the ferry.
That morning storm clouds were gathering and, as
a stranger on Orkney, he was unused to the twists
and turns of the currents in Wyre Sound.

Nancy of Hullion saw the storm beginning as she
was boiling a kettle for tea. Taking the kettle off
the hob, she ran to Hullion pier to greet the storm.
The next day she told Jael what she had seen.

'I was welcoming the thunder and lightning,' she
said, 'when I saw a boat drifting in Wyre Sound. In
it was Leo of the Norselands begging the storm to

abate, so he could find Wyre and the puffins on it to make a wedding dress for his bride. The more he begged, the more the storm whirled about him – till it smashed his boat on Egilsay rock.'

Jael gasped in horror. 'Do not fear lass,' Nancy continued. 'When the boat broke up, I saw Leo change into a walrus and swim to Egilsay for safety. His body will never be found, I'm telling you.'

And sure enough, though fragments of Leo's wrecked boat drifted back to Rousay, his body has not been seen to this day.

Leo's disappearance didn't deter suitors from coming to Trumland Castle to court Jael. Word had it that she was a wicked Princess in league with the devil. But as soon as the suitors saw her, they were bewitched. They saw that she was a wilful, passionate woman and not a wicked person at all.

Her suitors fancied that her hair, curling thickly down her back, had the fragrance of summer jasmine, and that her lips, if they could kiss them, would taste of summer pudding. Others said that clematis grew from her feet wherever she wandered on the island.

Magnus was the only man in Orkney not enchanted by Jael. 'Can't you hurry up and get married?' he begged her, his passion for Jewel close to capsizing. 'I really can't wait much longer!'

'Leave her be!' Jewel exclaimed. 'I'm sure Jael will pick a man soon, won't you my darling?'

Jael scowled, wishing in her heart that her sister and Magnus would shut up and leave her alone.

A week or so later, a fairy Prince arrived at Trumland Castle from the land of the Gauls. His name was Alvere. He came riding a white stallion, his golden hair blowing in the breeze. He brought with him gifts of figs and peaches, champagne and truffles. Jael rather liked him. She liked the way Alvere sang to her at night, and wrote poems calling her eyes, 'bright stars sparkling in the Orcadian night.'

Jael's heart trembled whenever he was near and when he reached out at last to touch her, she shook with smiles. Although she liked the idea of life eating peaches and drinking champagne all day long in the land of the Gauls, Jael didn't care for the slight sneer in Alvere's eyes or the downward turn of his thin lips when he smiled.

'I will marry you,' Jael said eventually, 'if you can jump the peaks of Boland and Brendale.'

Alvere laughed. He was renowned for his physical prowess and believed it would be simple to jump the peaks, even though belching between them was a perilous bog of quicksand and peat.

Alvere put on his silken sports clothes. He glowed in shimmering pink – a healthy, self-assured, sophisticated, fairy Prince. 'Be waiting in the wedding dress I brought for you when I return,' Alvere ordered Jael, before he started the journey to Boland and Brendale peaks.

The whole of Rousay turned out to see Alvere make his jump.

Nancy of Hullion and her black cat were there, Lord Blackhamar and his son Magnus, the King

and Princess Jewel, and all the island's crofters
and fishermen.

Now, the distance between the two peaks was fif-
teen feet, an easy enough distance for a fit man to
jump. But Alvere was so confident of himself that
he didn't bother to run into his jump fast enough.
He sauntered along, pirouetting daintily. To make
matters worse, he tripped just before his jump and
plunged head first into the perilous bog of Boland
and Brendale.

He would have been sucked straight into the un-
derworld if Nancy of Hullion hadn't hastily muttered
a charm that turned him into a pink flamingo. The
bird rose squawking from the bog and, flapping its
shining wings, flew away, far from Orkney.

Everybody had just about given up hope of Jael
ever marrying, when a gypsy Prince arrived on
Rousay. He said he was a Prince from Al-Andalus
on the Iberian Peninsular and that his name was
Kasim. On his arm was seated a magnificent golden
eagle whose eyes glittered with an intensity resem-
bling Jael's. Kasim's face was the colour of berries,
his lips the purple of amethysts and his eyes the
green of new emeralds. His mouth, when he smiled,
shone with the brilliance of a Seville sky in spring.

Jael's heart leapt when she saw him. She was about
to ask him to perform one of her famous tasks,
when he silenced her with a wave of his hand.

'Princess,' he said. 'I have travelled far to find someone to marry. I've journeyed from Al-Andalus to the Orient, and from the Norselands to Orkney. The woman I shall marry must be able to hold this eagle painlessly on her wrist. None of the Princesses that I've come across so far have been able to do this. Will you try, Orcadian Princess?'

Jael held out her hand. The golden eagle swooped down from the Prince's arm, landing on her wrist. It settled effortlessly, as if returning home at last. The bird's sharp claws didn't leave a single blemish on Jael's skin.

Looking rather shy, Kasim asked, 'Will you marry me?'

'Yes,' Jael replied. 'But on one condition. You must never ask me to be other than what I am. I am a woman who walks by night and listens to the music of the stars. I will marry you, but you must remember that my heart beats to its own rhythm and sings its own songs. Do you understand?'

The Prince said that he did and, taking Jael gently by the hand, they began the journey back to Al-Andalus.

Of course, everybody in Orkney was jubilant. Elaborate preparations were quickly made for Magnus's marriage to Jewel on Rousay. Musicians came over from Wyre for the wedding, and a priest from Eynhallow. The crofters and fishermen and

Nancy and her black cat danced till late the next morning, when more whisky and tea were served, and Magnus carried Jewel off to bed. At last Orkney had a son and heir.

And they say that, on that afternoon, a golden eagle flew three times around the north-west tower of Trumland Castle before turning southwards and flying back to Al-Andalus.

3

The Walrus Prince

This is the story of Prince Leo, who left his home to find a wife and was never seen or heard of again. Leo, the eldest son of Gustav, a King of the Norselands, was a kind, generous Prince with hair the colour of ripe wheat and eyes the brilliant blue of cornflowers. Leo's friendly manner made him popular with everyone who met him; however, the King, his father, was disappointed in his son.

'Not every man can be born a Viking,' said Queen Astrid to Gustav. 'Not every man likes to fight and pillage and make merry all night long. Some men are drawn to the finer things of life. Leo happens to be one of them.' Queen Astrid, who was manicuring her nails, flung back her strawberry-blonde hair as she dipped her fingers in a lotion of beeswax and lavender to soften her hands.

The King grunted, reluctant to argue with his wife.

The King's problem was that, although Leo was the eldest of his three sons, the young man didn't behave appropriately. That is, he didn't stride about – like the other men in the King's court – with long, strutting steps, and he didn't thump his chest and bellow when he laughed. What's more, Leo didn't enjoy jousting on horseback. To the King's dismay, his son had no talent, whatsoever, for duelling with swords or for wielding a dagger in close combat. It was bad enough that Leo didn't behave as a true Viking should – fierce as an eagle but with the cunning of a snake – but what hurt the King the most was that Leo simply didn't care.

In fact, the only sharp instruments he enjoyed holding were the kitchen knives he used for creating recipes with the Queens's chef and a pair of old secateurs for pruning roses in the Queen's garden. Most humiliating of all, unless it was as calm and still as a village pond, Leo was *petrified* of the sea.

The king shuddered at his son's peculiar behaviour, cringing at the thought that he, Gustav, a King of the Norselands, could have produced such a lily-livered man.

'Recipes and flowers indeed! And he's fearful of the sea. There isn't a Viking alive who doesn't love the sea!' Gustav mumbled into his beard as Astrid rubbed sprigs of rosemary into her hair to clean and perfume it. 'This is Astrid's doing. If she didn't dote on Leo so, if she didn't make such a fuss of the boy, he wouldn't be such a disgrace.'

***

At last, when Leo had given up sword play and wrestling altogether and refused to set foot on a boat, Red Norman, a messenger from the King of Orkney, arrived at Gustav's court with a message. Gustav listened carefully to the messenger from the Orcadian King and, as he did so, an idea seeded in his mind. If he could behave with the ruthlessness of a true Viking, if he could only hold his nerve, he knew that before long his problem with his eldest son would be solved. Without further ado, Gustav ordered that the very next evening a banquet would be held in the Great Hall in honour of Red Norman of Rousay. And at the banquet, Gustav, a King of the Norselands would make an important announcement.

There was nothing more pleasing to Leo than preparing for a royal banquet at short notice. He quickly sharpened his cooking knives and then, in collaboration with the Queen's chef, prepared a menu for the sumptuous feast which they cooked the next day. Ten maid-servants helped them in the kitchen and on the evening of the banquet, serving girls streamed out of the royal kitchens carrying cauldrons of creamy lobster soup. They brought out trays of crab-meat on rye bread, followed by platters of cured salmon seasoned with dill and spice. For pudding there was cloudberry pie served with thimbles of cloudberry liqueur, that reminded those sipping it of the first hint of autumn after long days of midsummer sun. Everyone present relished the meal. When they had eaten their fill and were salting their tongues on coils of liquorice, Leo brought out his harp and sang.

The voice that came out of the King's eldest son was strong and melodious. What's more it was reassuring, even though the song Leo sang brought to mind a blue moon on a star-tossed night. Leo sang about lost love and sad farewells. He sang with all his heart, so that it seemed to Queen Astrid that his voice glittered – darting and flashing like the Northern Lights. Astrid blushed, delighted, while the down growing in the crease of the King's back stiffened.

Gustav pushed back his chair and stood up. 'I have an announcement to make,' he said, bringing Leo's singing to a halt. 'An announcement!'

Before Gustav could say any more, the guests in the Great Hall burst into rapturous applause – not for the King but for Leo.

'A toast!' someone shouted. 'A toast for Prince Leo!'

There was loud thumping of chests, the raising of glasses and drunken roars of 'Encore! Bravo! Another song, Leo!'

'I have an announcement to make,' the King thundered.

Gradually, everyone fell silent. Everyone, that is, except for the Queen, who was asking one of her ladies-in-waiting to fetch a glass of fruit cordial to soothe Leo's throat.

'As you know already,' said Gustav, 'this banquet is in honour of Red Norman, who is here on behalf of the King of Orkney. What none of you are aware of is the important message Norman has brought with him.' The King paused to gulp down some liqueur, thrilled that everyone wanted to hear more.

Gustav growled and coughed. He took another swig of cloudberry, and smiled bashfully at his son. 'Orkney wants it to be known,' he said at last, 'that he's looking for husbands for three of his daughters. I've decided to send Leo to woo them. It would be to our advantage if the ties between the Norselands and Orkney were cemented in marriage.'

Leo's brothers patted him on the back as if he'd already returned home with an Orcadian bride. They didn't seem to notice that their brother looked on bewildered.

'I want you to go, Leo,' the King said, 'because I'm convinced that marriage will be the making of you. Only a true Viking can win the heart of an Orkney Princess, so you must become a true Viking indeed!'

At these words the Queen grew pale. Her fingers fumbled with a silver pendant around her neck and as she stared at the King, the glaze of tears in her eyes brought a chill to his heart.

Clutching the pendant, the Queen rose unsteadily to her feet. 'May Leo return safely with a wife who will love him always,' she declared. 'A wife who can see him for what he is: a strong, gentle man, the sweetest and most loving of men!' Then, raising her glass, the Queen drank a toast to her son.

The King decided that Prince Leo would leave Norway with Red Norman by the end of the week. Leo hastily put his affairs in order and on the morning of his departure went to the Queen's chamber to say goodbye.

'I've a feeling your journey is going to be difficult,' the Queen said, touching Leo's cheek. 'Perhaps we shan't see each other again. So before you leave, I want to remind you that nature has made you a patient man, Leo. You are patient and caring, yet there are some women who can't be won with patience, my dear. Don't be disheartened. I believe that after you've passed through great danger, you'll find true love.'

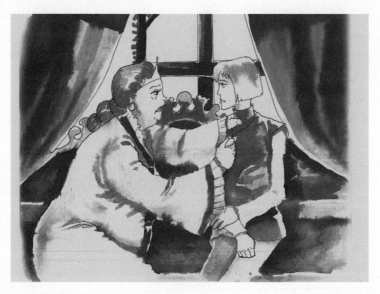

'I don't want to go,' Leo sighed. 'I want to stay with you here, mother.'

Unable to bear the sight of tears welling up in her son's eyes, the Queen turned away to hold back her own tears. When she was herself again, Astrid faced her son: 'The world isn't always a happy place, Leo. At times like this, it seems very dismal indeed. Remember how much I love you and heed what I'm going to tell you.'

Astrid stroked the token to Freya – the goddess of love, who soars through the heavens on a chariot hauled by black cats – she wore around her neck. 'Remember that the sea is your friend, my son. At times, she can be as jealous as a woman determined to claim you as her own. But she can also soothe you, Leo, and reward you. You may not realise this but if you make friends with her, she'll look after you. And when your time of danger comes, remember, ask her for help and she'll protect you.'

Drawing her son closer, the Queen kissed him before handing him the locket of Freya to wear in her memory.

***

For over a year, Leo was a guest at Trumland Castle – home of the King of Orkney. His gentle ways made him a favourite with the four Princesses, who listened enraptured to the stories he sang with his harp. Delilah and Jezebel tossed teasing glances in his direction, but it was Jael that Leo loved. He was drawn to the glint of midnight in her eyes, and when she smiled at him, that hint of tenderness on her face that showed that she liked him.

The Prince waited patiently until the two eldest Princesses were married before approaching Jael. Then, on the first day of summer, when the sun was out on Rousay and the wind was soft as a baby's sigh, Leo made a crown of pansies for the Princess.

'Heartsease,' he murmured, placing the wreath on Jael's head. 'Will you ease my heart, sweet Princess, by doing me the honour of marrying me?'

Jael roared with laughter, shaking so violently that she split a seam of her red dress, revealing a ribbon of flesh.

'O Leo!' she squirmed, dabbing her eyes with a sleeve. 'Please don't go wobbly on me like the rest of those fools. You're my friend, you idiot! Don't make me throw you off the island like I've done all the others.'

Undeterred, Leo trailed behind Jael – a pale, faithful Labrador.

Later that morning he fed her cakes he'd baked in the royal kitchens, cakes made of apple and carrot and walnut. Then, in the afternoon, he made her a bouquet of wild poppies with blue-eyed borage and red campion. And when Leo's heart was full to overflowing, he rubbed the silver locket he wore and asked of Freya: 'Why doesn't she love me? Why doesn't Jael of Orkney love me and go back to the Norselands with me as my bride?'

As dusk fell and the island of Rousay, bathed in grey pearly light, shimmered in the sea, Leo pleaded with Jael to reconsider his offer. She turned her back on him yet again. Dejected, Leo sang out his sorrow to the sea in a voice so clear and true that the rocks around Rousay shivered when they heard his song.

Jael, however, was still unmoved. In fact, the next day, when the two of them went for a walk on Scaqouy Head, she warned Leo never to speak of marriage again. But Leo couldn't help himself. Before dusk had fallen, he proposed once again.

'Is that man simple?' Jael's other suitors muttered to each other as they saw Leo emerging from the royal kitchens with a tray of fairy cakes for the Princess. 'Can't he see that he'll never win her love? Can't he see that his case is hopeless and he should move over to make room for us?'

That's what they said. And yet, while countless suitors were dismissed from the island and rejected outright, Leo was allowed to stay – as long as he behaved the way Jael wanted.

At last the day came when Leo discovered the Princess prowling the garden of Trumland Castle. She paced between the rose bushes, catching her dress on thorns. Every now and again she shook the dress loose, leaving a trail of rose petals behind her.

Leo picked one up and placed it against his cheek. It was from a bush his mother loved, a wild rambling rose, which grew in pink clusters against the west wall of her summer house in Norseland. 'This petal is an omen from Freya,' Leo thought. 'An omen that my time has come.'

The Prince blocked Jael's path, placed a hand on her shoulder, and asked for the third time: 'Will you marry me, Orkney Princess?'

'Blast you, Leo!'

Leo thought he was about to be slapped but to his surprise, after scrutinising him, Jael said petulantly, 'Very well, Leo of Norseland. I'll marry you. But first you must make me a wedding dress from the feathers of puffins.'

Leo was overjoyed. 'I'll do anything you want, Jael, anything at all. Nothing will give me greater pleasure than to find feathers to adorn you for our wedding. The goddess of love glides through the sky in a cloak made of hawk's wings.'

With those words Leo ran to find a boat to sail to Wyre Island where a colony of puffins lived. 'When

I come back,' he promised the Princess, 'with the help of Freya, my love for you will be such that you will love me in return.'

***

If he'd had more sense, Leo would have waited for the ferry to Wyre that morning, instead of rushing off. But eager to marry Jael and return home quickly after a year on Rousay, he brushed aside his usual nervousness around water and leapt into a rowing boat, paddling furiously towards Wyre. He didn't notice storm clouds gathering, and as a stranger to Orkney he didn't yet understand the curious ways of the Rousay currents. Leo was in love and in too much of a hurry to notice that anything was wrong. Until, halfway between Wyre and Rousay, a clap of thunder rocked the sea and turbulent waves thrust him off course towards the island of Egilsay – an island ringed by sharp granite rocks.

Wet and shivering, Leo cried out as lightening tore open the sky to reveal the faces of goblins laughing at him. The thunder roared again, this time with a low, ominous rumble, as if the mere sight of Leo struggling on the sea made it angry.

Terrified, the Prince called out a second time as the wind swept the boat towards the rocks off Egilsay. 'Wind and rain stop!' he begged. 'Stop! For I must go to Wyre to make a dress of puffin's feathers for my Orkney bride.'

If the storm heard Leo, it failed to respond. It flung the boat closer to Egilsay. Leo thrust the oars against a slab of rock to push himself to safety but first one and then the second oar snapped as the boat flooded with water. Convinced that he was about to die, the Prince clutched the locket around his neck to sing a last song.

His voice rose, a church bell sounding through the storm, through lashing rain and biting gale.

Leo sang for his family in the Norselands, the tall pines and glaciers of his home. Then, he sang for Jael whose careless love had led him to his fate. The gale seemed to answer him in Astrid's voice: a mother's howl of grief as her son, his boat smashing against rocks, begins his journey from one world to the next.

'Mother, is that you?' Leo asked the wind. 'Are you there?'

Believing that he could hear his mother's voice, Leo remembered what she had said as she kissed him goodbye. Leo remembered her words and begged the sea for mercy.

The wind and rain paid no heed to his plea but the sea, sensing his desperation, stilled her waves. Having listened to Leo's songs over the past year and been soothed by them, she swallowed him deep down into her belly.

At first, Leo didn't know what was happening to him. Swaddled in an element he detested, he thought he was drowning, being swept towards a watery grave, when all at once the sea seemed to cradle him, buoying him, till he floated up to see the sky again.

The storm had passed, the air was still, and yet Leo felt completely different. He *was* different. He saw that his skin, which had been white as the snow on the mountains of the Norselands, though still pale, was rough as a pumice stone. His hands, which had once teased tunes from a harp, were clumsy, fat flippers. His feet were large fins. What's more, his beautiful golden hair had gone, replaced by a stubble of bristles on his chin. Leo would not have recognised himself had it not been for his mother's silver locket coiled around one of the two tusks that sprang from where his teeth had been.

'Has it come to this? Have I become a walrus?' he asked, refusing to believe what his eyes told him. 'Is this hulk what has become of Leo of the Norselands?'

Leo's tears fell on Egilsay rock. They fell until the granite crags glistened beneath the midday sun. As always, sadness moved Leo to sing. He raised his curved tusks to the sky and opened his mouth to give his sorrow to the sea. He cleared his throat and breathed in deeply but instead of a glorious voice ringing out clear and true, a large croak came out. Leo sounded like an old Viking burping after a heavy meal.

'What has become of my voice?' He opened his mouth again to sing but the same undignified noise rang out louder than a donkey's fart.

'Not only have I become a walrus, I've also lost the gift I treasure most. My home is the sea, yet I've never liked the sea. I much prefer living on land. Not that I'm ungrateful, mind you ...'

The pools of Egilsay rock rose as Leo filled them
with his tears. They rose till they covered the tip of
the highest granite peak and ran into the sea. The
people of Rousay saw the island of Egilsay disap-
pear under a river of tears. On the nearby island
of Wyre, the white puffins whose feathers Jael had
wanted for her wedding dress, scattered in alarm.
Finally, the people of Rousay saw a fat grey walrus,
its head bowed in grief, slowly swim away.

***

Leo travelled to the lands of the north to find
creatures that looked like him: creatures with skins
as tough as elephants and faces wizened by the
wind. After several days, he came across a family
of walruses looking for food beside the island of
Greenland. They welcomed Leo into their circle,
nibbling the stubble on his chin in greeting.

'How did you get that silver locket around your
tusk?' asked a curious young walrus who hadn't
yet grown tusks. He was anxious to know the
background of the wandering walrus that had just
joined them.

'I'm not really one of you,' Leo confessed, stifling
a sob. 'I'm Leo – a Prince of the Norselands. I went
to Orkney to find a wife and became as I am when
the sea saved my life.'

'You don't seem very pleased to be alive,' grunted an old bull walrus with long, grey bristles on his chin.

'I don't feel at home at sea,' Leo replied. 'I prefer dry land. What's more, since my change, I've lost my voice. I can't sing anymore and I love singing.'

'Of course you can't sing like those humans do,' explained the old bull walrus. 'We walruses don't sing that type of song. We have our own music.'

His relatives nodded in agreement.

'But I love singing,' said Leo. 'Even more than I love cooking and gardening. Singing makes me who I am.'

'Who you were,' said the old walrus, shaking his head sadly.

'You'll not be able to sing as a walrus, I'm afraid. Not unless you find your voice again or find a mate. Then you'll sing a walrus song, which will be the making of you.'

The family of walruses waddled around Leo to comfort him. They stroked his back, massaging it softly to make him feel better. As they rubbed and stroked and grunted and snuffled, they put their heads together to think of a plan to help the walrus Prince.

'We could take him back to Orkney to search for his old voice there,' one suggested.

'We could look inside a conch shell,' said another. 'They hold the music of the sea.'

'I have the answer,' said the old walrus, grunting in excitement.

'Whale can help. The whale who travels with the fish-woman. The woman who once walked on land.'

Quickly, the old walrus told Leo about Ajuba, the fisherman's daughter, who had been sent to sea by her village and had become a mermaid. Ajuba swam the seven seas with her best friend Whale, who occasionally returned to Greenland to visit relatives.

'Whale should be coming home shortly,' explained the walrus, 'and when she does, I'll ask her to take you to the fisherman's daughter. If anyone can help you, I'm sure she can.'

For seven days Leo waited for Whale to appear.
He waited with the family of walruses who tried
their best to make him feel at home in the sea.
They lazed about in the warm summer sunshine,
splashing in the waters of Greenland. They guz-
zled clams and crabs, then feasted on sea-worms
tossed with sea cucumbers and cabbage. In the
afternoon they relaxed on cushions of seaweed,
burping happily to the sun.

If it hadn't been for the fact that he could no
longer sing, Leo might have tolerated his new life
in his ungainly new body. The mounds of blubber
beneath his skin, which had turned pinkish-brown
in the sun, kept him gloriously warm in icy water.
And day by day, he began to realise that his lum-
bering bulk made him less anxious about being in
water. It was the sea that had saved him and now,
when he plunged in the element he'd once been
frighted of, instead of feeling cold and clumsy, he
was graceful and at ease.

No, life as a walrus wasn't bad; especially since Leo
was enjoying spending time with a big-eyed walrus
who had taken a liking to him. As she scrubbed
and pummelled his back, the frustrations of his
stay on Rousay were rubbed away and, gradually,
Leo forgot his love for Jael.

At the end of a week, Leo bade farewell to the walruses and swam towards an iceberg where he'd been

told that Whale would be waiting for him. When she saw Leo, Whale looked at him suspiciously.

'Why do you want to meet my friend Ajuba?' she asked, wary of anyone who might intrude on her friendship with the fisherman's daughter or anyone who might hurt her.

'I need help to find my voice,' Leo said. 'I lost it when I became a walrus and I'm not at all happy without it.'

'I'm not sure that Ajuba's the person you're after. I'm not sure if anyone can help you for that matter.'

The look of desolation that swept over Leo's grizzled face at the suggestion that no one might be able to help him surprised Whale. So much so that, being a fundamentally kind-hearted creature, she added quickly: 'I'm not *sure* if Ajuba will be able to help you, but maybe it'll be worth your while talking to her.'

'Pray tell me, where does my lady dwell?'

'I left *my lady* in the Gulf of Siam. *Your lady*,' Whale sniffed, 'is with a band of sea gypsies. She says they're worshipping her – though how pouring bottles of whisky and lotus flower wine into the sea can be described as worship I don't know. I'm happy to take you to her if that's what you want. But whether it'll do you any good or not . . .'

'I need to meet her,' Leo insisted. 'I don't think I have any other choice at the moment.'

And so it was that with a swish of their tails, the walrus Prince and Whale began the long journey to the Gulf of Siam.

**

They travelled across the choppy waters of the Bay of Biscay, around the coast of Africa, to the emerald land of Siam where the people live by an inner grace directed by the sea and stars. There, they discovered Ajuba floating on warm water, her face turned up to the sun.

Up till that moment, Leo, having only been a walrus for a short time, had never seen a mermaid. He was startled by what he saw. Ajuba was almost as tall as Whale. Her skin shone like polished black coral and her long fish's tail, which could move with the strength of a herd of sea lions, swished seductively in the turquoise water.

The fisherman's daughter gave the walrus Prince a lazy smile of welcome and, as she did so, Leo sensed that if anyone could help him find his voice again then Ajuba was that person.

'Well,' she said, when she'd listened to Leo's story, 'I think the first thing we must do is investigate your talent for singing. When you walked on land, what did people say your voice was like?'

Leo paused to think. Eventually, he said: 'At times they used to say that I sang like a nightingale. I've also heard it said that my voice is like a tinkling silver bell. But my mother claims that when I sing she is enchanted, overcome with the magical splendour of the Northern Lights.'

'Anything else?' Ajuba probed, sensitive to the wobble in Leo's voice when he mentioned his mother.

The walrus Prince snuffled. 'Sometimes,' he sighed, 'when I was really inspired, people used to say that it was as if I was singing to Freya – the goddess of love. They said I used to sing to her with the voice of a bird born in paradise,'

'A bird of paradise,' Ajuba murmured, scratching her scalp to help her think. 'I'm not sure about this, but it's worth a try ...'

Without further ado she dived underwater, cutting through currents to the boats of the sea gypsies. The gypsy children hailed her, calling to their parents to come and look at the black goddess. Soon the decks were crowded with people throwing paper flowers at Ajuba. There were old men and women, naked brown children, men wrapped in sarongs, and sun-kissed women suckling their babies.

Ajuba silenced them with a wave of her hand. 'I want you to do something for me,' she asked, as a hush descended over the honey-brown people. 'Will you fetch me the feathers of birds of paradise?

Twenty-one glorious feathers; one for every year the walrus Prince has lived.'

Delighted to do the bidding of their ebony goddess, the sea gypsies pulled up anchor and sailed away in their brightly coloured boats. A warm wind blew them gently along the coast until they arrived at their destination: a sheltered cove that led to a jungle on the mainland of Siam.

When night fell, a group of gypsies waded to shore guided by the fluorescence of the sea and the light of the stars. They each carried a birdcage, for they knew that in the jungle – in the safety of quiet glades where fruit and flowers grew – lived many birds of paradise.

The gypsies placed the cages on the forest floor, leaving a trail of sweetened nuts to every door. At a signal from their leader, they retreated to the shadows to wait for their prey. Before long, they heard a bird of paradise singing. And then a second bird and a third – their voices shining in the air with the brilliance of fireflies.

As the first bird hopped closer, its song filled the glade with a thread of golden sound that made the leaves of trees tremble, while insects vibrated in chorus. A second bird, then a third, dropped to the forest floor and, between bursts of song, they nibbled the nuts and pecked their way into captivity.

By dawn, every single one of the twenty-one cages
was filled with a bird beating its wings against bars.

Anxious not to prolong their captivity, the leader
of the gypsies plucked a tail feather from each of
them before allowing them to fly free again. The
birds flew into the air, their wings lighting up the
morning sky.

***

The sea gypsies returned to the Gulf of Siam to
find Ajuba tickling the walrus Prince with a palm
leaf. Leo croaked happily between chuckles. Then,
diving underwater, he circled Ajuba. As he did so,
he made walrus sounds: a clicking and drumming
from the back of his mouth, a strange, rhythmic
music that walruses make when they find a mate.
Though his body was still cumbersome, it didn't
seem to matter anymore; with Ajuba at his side,
Leo felt beautiful again – alive and gifted with love.

'Do you want these feathers?' the captain of the
sea gypsies called out to Ajuba.

'Do you still want your voice back?' Ajuba asked
Leo.

The walrus Prince nodded, and so Ajuba wove a
necklace with the twenty-one feathers. She twisted the necklace around Leo's neck, then wound
it around his tusks so that, intertwined with his

mother's locket, it hung as a garland fluttering on Leo's chest.

'Try and sing something now,' Ajuba suggested.

Leo cleared his throat and opened his mouth, filling his lungs with a deep breath, the way he'd always done before singing at King Gustav's castle. Leo cleared his throat again. He coughed. Then, after filling his lungs a second time, he opened his mouth and the silver-feathered necklace snapped.

An unearthly sound filled the Gulf of Siam. It rose like a wave sweeping across the shore to herald the sun and moon laughing at each other across the sky. Yet it wasn't a frightening noise, for the sea gypsies who heard it say it was as sweet as a rainbow dripping honey.

To their amazement, they watched the walrus Prince become a man again: a man with the torso of a prince and the tail of an enormous kingfish. They say they saw the walrus Prince swim with their black goddess and a whale far out to sea. And they say (though how they know this I'm not sure) that in a cold faraway kingdom of pine trees and glaciers, a Queen called Astrid heard the walrus Prince's song, and knew that her son was happy at last.

4

Romilly The Golden Eagle

No one would have thought when Romilly of Westray married Cullen the Carouser, King of Orkney, that her life would be anything but happy. During the marriage ceremony, as the couple exchanged vows before the priests of Eynhallow, the old dowagers of Orkney wiped away tears at the sight of Romilly. The look of love on the new Queen's face made her shine and when she declared 'I do' for all to hear, it seemed that everything about her – her dress with its long silken veil, the blush of pearls that adorned her, even the garland of flowers on her head – glowed in adoration of the King.

The dowagers sighed, remembering their own wedding celebrations when they too had been young brides full of hope. 'Aye, it looks easy enough,' they muttered. 'It's easy enough to love and marry but to stay happy beside a wilful Orcadian is another matter altogether.'

The first three years of Romilly's life as Queen were happy ones. She decorated Trumland Castle on the island of Rousay, where she lived with the King, to her liking. The moth-eaten skins that hung on the walls were replaced with bright tapestries of fantastic creatures. Soon dragons, unicorns and sea horses danced on the walls of the Great Hall and feathers that she gathered on her wanderings around the island decorated her bedroom mirror.

She filled the damp, dreary castle with the sound of singing canaries, the bloom of everlasting flowers. And in every room she made a potpourri of lavender and jasmine, insisting that, no matter what the weather was outside, every hearth in the castle should be kept alight to make her home as warm as possible.

The King doted on his Queen. He said her smile was like the first breath of spring after a long Orcadian winter, her laugh as bright as fireflies at night. He loved her so much that one morning he presented her with a golden tray of peaches and figs, delicacies rarely seen in Orkney.

'Here's a peach for every son you're going to give me,' the King said, patting Romilly's fair hair.

'But that's eight! Don't you want any daughters, Cullen?'

'Perhaps one to keep you company, dear,' the King replied. 'Orkney needs sons to keep away troublemakers, sons to maintain the traditions of Trumland Castle. You do understand don't you, Romilly?'

Laughing as she savoured every bite of the peach, the Queen wiped away a trickle of juice dribbling down her chin.

'What children men are,' she said later to Betsy, her old nursemaid. 'What if I give birth to daughters? Eight sons indeed!'

Betsy, braiding her mistress's hair, spoke to the Queen's reflection. The image, pale and ghostly in the glass, was framed by feathers Romilly had collected on her walks. Feathers of robins and blackbirds, along with feathers of birds that soared over the hills of Orkney – buzzards, kites and clear-eyed eagles.

'They're children who can't be spanked, that's what men are! And if you spoil them like you do the King, Ma'am, they insist on having their way all the time. And then, when they don't get what they want . . .'

'That's quite enough, thank you,' said Romilly, snatching her long, thick plait from Betsy to tie herself.

The Queen didn't like being continually reminded by Betsy of the many ways she indulged her boisterous husband. She allowed him to practice archery in the Great Hall, and to run up and down the castle corridors at night throwing lighted torches to his drinking companions. She allowed Cullen the Carouser and his men to do this even though sometimes, in their revelry, they set her tapestries alight.

'My husband isn't perfect,' the Queen sighed after one such incident. She had come downstairs that morning to find her favourite tapestry, of a white unicorn garlanded with roses, badly singed. Romilly chose to ignore it. Biting her tongue, she turned away to gaze at the calm waters of Rousay. 'I know he isn't perfect. But then who in this world is without fault? Cullen is wilful, at times he's reckless and unpredictable, but I love him. And as long as he loves me in return, I can't help giving in to him, no matter what Betsy says.'

Before long the Queen was expecting a baby. The King, eager to become a father, began preparing his friends for the talents of his future son.

'He'll be the best huntsman in Orkney,' he told Lord Blackhamar as he downed a tot of whisky. 'He'll chase deer and wild boar and women as well. And catch 'em, I'll wager.'

The two men nudged each other and chortled. Betsy, knitting woollens for the baby in a corner of the Great Hall, sniffed indignantly.

'And he'll run faster than a hare,' the King boasted to Red Norman, his bearded messenger.

Norman agreed, refilling their glasses.

'Let's hope he's not like Leo, the King of Norseland's son,' said Blackhamar grinning. 'Now that's a poor son for a Viking to have. Cries at a glimspe of the sea, and hates salt water with a vengeance, he does. No good to man or beast.'

'The child may be a girl,' said a quiet voice. Romilly, seated by the fire, was embroidering peacock feathers on a silk shawl for her baby. 'The child may be strong and agile but a girl all the same.'

'Nonsense!' bellowed Cullen the Carouser. Then, remembering his love for his Queen, he walked to her side and patted her tenderly on the head.

When the baby was born, it was a girl with sparkling eyes and ruby lips. The King was too awed to be angry. He gazed down at his daughter, prodding her to make sure she was alive. The baby wriggled in her peacock-feather shawl and opened herself up to her father.

'She'll get her way this one, like I do. Look at her eyes, Romilly,' said the King. 'She has the eyes of a Jezebel, a beautiful Jezebel. Yes, that's what I'll call her.'

The Queen laughed, relieved that despite what he had said previously the King liked the child.

'She's not as good as a boy mind you,' her husband added, reading her thoughts. 'But I can see

the girl has character. Our next bairn had better
be a boy though. It will be a boy, won't it Romilly?'

Romilly's second child was another daughter, born
with an auburn curl twisting down her forehead,
a smile playing on her lips. Betsy wrapped her up
carefully in a kingfisher wrap the Queen had embroidered, and showed the baby to the King.

'Isn't she gorgeous?' Betsy cooed.

'She'll lead men astray, that one,' he replied, looking suspiciously at his daughter. 'She's a Delilah,
if ever I saw one. Romilly, when are you going to
give me a son?' he demanded. 'More than anything
in the world, I want a son!'

Romilly looked helplessly at her husband. 'I'd like
a son too,' she sighed. 'But I can't defy nature's
will. Why aren't you satisfied with what we've got,
Cullen? We've got two beautiful, healthy daughters.'

'I need a son!' the King shouted. 'A son for Orkney!'

The King's obsession with an heir cast a shadow
over Romilly's life at Trumland Castle. Her husband
grew unruly, neglecting his family to spend time
with his friends, chieftains of the Orkney clans.
Lord Blackhamar and Erik the Skull-splitter were
frequent visitors at the castle, as were Edgar, Ivan
and Cuthbert, the three brothers from Cogar. They
sang and drank till late into the night, making such
a noise that travellers passing outside hurried along,
convinced that the castle was possessed by demons.

'This will never do,' said Betsy to her mistress's reflection, as she transformed the Queen's hair into a mass of curls. 'No! Those men weren't content to stay in the Great Hall last night. Not those merrymakers! They had to sing and dance along the west corridor, waking the little Princesses. No Ma'am,' she said shaking her head severely, 'this will never do.'

Romilly's answer was to sit by a window and gaze out to sea. 'My husband is unhappy,' she decided. 'I try to soothe him but I can't because the sight of me with our daughters reminds him of his need for a son. I irritate him, yet he loves me still. I *know* he still loves me.'

She picked up a white silk shawl she had started embroidering. On it she was stitching a pattern of raven's feathers, dark swords clashing against each other. Romilly was expecting another child, you see, and she knew it was another girl.

When the baby was born and the King saw her, he decided to call her Jael – for the baby's penetrating eyes seemed to cut right through him. It was as if the child glimpsed that, with the arrival of yet another daughter, the King's love for his Queen was dwindling. He seemed to swallow it with the whisky he drank to ease his longing for a son. And yet he found peace nowhere.

Eyes that had once looked tenderly at Romilly became sullen and cloudy, indifferent to her beauty and cold to her warmth. Days went by without the King saying a word to his Queen. Then, one morning, remembering the passion of his youth and the vows he had made in church, Cullen the Carouser forgot his sorrow and gathered Romilly in his arms again.

'I would do anything to please you, Cullen,' the Queen assured him. 'Anything at all ...'

The King hugged his wife tightly. But after loving her, he shunned her. To Romilly's dismay that very evening he was distant and resorted to ridiculing her in front of their friends.

'As for my *Queen*,' he jeered, 'the only bairns she's able to push out are girls. I'll have to take my pleasure elsewhere to have me a son.'

Such poisonous words of contempt brought tears to Romilly's eyes.

'Stop looking at me like that, woman!' cried Cullen.'Get away from me and take those brats with you!'

To the embarrassment of everyone present – Blackhamar, Erik and the three brothers from Cogar – the Queen left the room sobbing. It seemed the only love the King was able to express was that which he showed his daughter Jael, who he insisted should be brought up as a boy.

The next day, humiliated and unhappy, Romilly wandered over the cliffs of Rousay and listened to the haunting call of seagulls. She walked over scrubland and rocks, adding to her collection of birds' feathers.

'This belongs to a cormorant,' she said, placing a moist, dark plume in the pocket of her cloak. 'And this is from a hawk.'

It was as if by scavenging over rough land, she was keeping alight her love for the King. And when she found another feather, she said: 'He loves me still. I know Cullen still loves me.'

That winter, the little Princesses and Betsy were the only people able to bring a smile to the Queen's face. Jezebel and Delilah drew pictures for their mother, while Jael, a fat toddler, sat on Romilly's lap stroking her golden hair.

One evening when the sky was night-blue and the children were getting ready for bed, they asked Romilly for a story. She told them of a King who brought a shining tray of peaches and figs to his Queen. The fruit tasted so good, she said, that ever after, whenever the Queen was sad, she remembered that tray of fruit.

'Did it make her feel better?' Delilah asked, a puzzled expression on her face.

The Queen nodded.

'But how?' Jezebel wanted to know.

'It helped her feel better,' Romilly replied, 'because it reminded her of how things used to be. And when she remembered, she knew that she would endure anything, anything at all, if the King could return to loving her once more.'

'Why did he stop loving her, Mama?' Jezebel continued.

Romilly sighed. 'Hush, my child,' she said. 'It's time you went to sleep. You too, Delilah.'

Just before the winter solstice, the Queen realised that she was expecting another baby and began embroidering yet another silk shawl. This one was inky-blue, the colour of a glittering sea at twilight. And on its border she stitched a crown of dove's feathers.

'This child will bring peace to my marriage,' she told herself. 'And if it is nature's will, the King will have a son at last.'

Outside, swollen by wind and rain, the Rousay sea tossed angrily against granite rocks. The winter storms were beginning.

One night, while the King was carousing with his friends in the Great Hall, the Queen went into labour. She didn't utter a word. She lay staring through a castle window, listening to the sea smashing against the rocks below.

Wind and rain splattered the window, sending chilly gusts of air into the chamber. The feathers around the Queen's mirror fluttered. At last, a baby was born. Another girl! Romilly looked sadly into the baby's face as she cradled it in her arms.

'You're my Jewel,' she murmured, kissing the child's soft crown. 'My precious Jewel.'

On hearing that he had another daughter, Cullen tugged his beard in despair. He gnashed his teeth, pulling at his clothes. They fell in shreds at his feet. Then, racing upstairs, he ran wildly through the castle, pounding on every door till he came to the Queen's chamber. There, unable to contain his fury, he broke down the door, and seeing Romilly's pale reflection in the feathered mirror, he raised his sword and struck.

The glass shattered into pieces and, as it did so, the beautiful feathers Romilly had gathered during her years on Rousay scattered on the floor.

'Be gone!' Cullen cried. 'I never want to see you again, Romilly! From now on you and your brats will live in the north-west tower of Trumland Castle.' With these words the King banished his wife from his life.

A time of great sorrow came to the Queen and the people of Orkney. The King forgot them to drink with his chieftains in the Great Hall. Refusing to govern, he allowed the island to fall into disrepair. He ignored his wife and forgot his daughters. All of them that is except for little Jael, the girl-son he adored.

The north-west tower held painful memories for Romilly. It was where she had lived with the King when they were newly-weds. The rooms were sumptuously decorated in red and gold, and the dark-blue ceilings shimmered with painted stars. As Jezebel and Delilah rolled on the floor over cushions where their parents had once lain, Betsy noticed the anguish on her mistress's face. She shooed the children away, telling them their mother needed as much peace and rest as possible.

But Romilly could not rest. She wandered through the red rooms of the north-west tower, remembering the King's gift of peaches and figs. It seemed such a long time ago. Even so, it was hard to believe that she was now little more than a prisoner in her husband's castle!

'He no longer loves me,' she mumbled as she paced up and down, ripping out her gorgeous hair. 'Cullen no longer loves me. Dear God, how am I to live if he no longer cares for me?'

Romilly trailed through the rooms without seeing her children. And if Betsy hadn't placed the new baby at her breast, the Queen would certainly have let it starve. The only thing she showed any interest in was what remained of her collection of feathers. One day, as she was playing with them absent-mindedly, Romilly stuck three feathers into her dishevelled hair.

'Now this won't do Ma'am,' said Betsy, tidying up her mistress. 'We can't have you turning yourself into a scarecrow, can we now? Why don't you sit by the window and do a bit of embroidery?'

The kindly woman kissed the Queen's cheek, smoothing her brow. The face, which till recently had been bright with memories, was now cold as marble. It was as if Romilly was dead to the world.

A moment later, when Betsy slipped out to attend to the children, Romilly opened the window and stepped out on to the turret roof. She didn't feel the wind and rain whipping against her, or the trail of tears flowing down her cheeks. All she knew was that the islanders of Orkney and her daughters were ill-used by her husband. And yet she could not live without his love. With her golden hair twisted around her neck, Romilly lent over the turret and flung herself down.

Just as she was about to hit the jagged rocks below, a feather still in her hair remembered it had once flown and twitched. Immediately the Queen was transformed into a bird, a huge golden eagle with strong wide wings. Beating them frantically, she flew upwards and circled Trumland Castle before flying away, far away towards the warmer climate of the south.

***

Romilly flew for miles over the stormy seas of Orkney. She flew at great speed, gliding with air currents over large expanses of land. She crossed mountains and hills, farmland marked with stone walls and countryside covered with hedgerows. She flew without stopping, relishing the new-found freedom that carried her far from Rousay with every beat of her wings.

As she swept over water, Romilly realised that her eagle eyes were able to penetrate the dark waves of the Atlantic. Deep down she saw lobsters and crabs scrabbling on the sea floor. Over land she caught the slightest flicker of movement from miles away.

'I like being a bird,' she decided, forging ahead beyond the land of the Gauls. 'Flying within the clouds is like dancing on vapour and gliding above them feels like kissing the sun.'

Romilly flew on and on until she reached a land of mountains surrounded by fertile valleys that sheltered villages. She wafted over groves of peaches, figs, olives and apricots and reached a town full of orange blossom – the city of Seville in Al-Andalus on the Iberian Peninsula.

Curious to take a closer look, Romilly circled the old Moorish palace – the Alcázar. As she did so, she heard a piercing whistle and drifted down. The palace falconer, Prince Kasim, was trying to entice her down. Romilly scrutinised him with her new eagle eyes, then peered at him with the wary intuition of a forsaken woman. When she sensed that the kindness evident in the Prince's eyes reflected the true nature of his heart, Romilly came down to him and settled on his outstreßtched arm.

The Prince took the golden eagle to an aviary, home of the royal hunting birds. In it were twelve falcons and ten kites. Kasim had always yearned to train an eagle, the most noble of birds, to hunt for him. He was amazed that the bird had come to him, for it was fully-grown and seemed wild.

He placed the eagle in the aviary, only to be met by screams of alarm as with outstretched wings the other birds scrambled into a corner, leaving the golden eagle by itself.

Very soon Kasim loved the eagle more than all the other birds in his care. He admired the regal way it held its head, the glorious colouring of its feathers. The bird's eyes seemed to pierce into his soul and it was able to understand him better than even the falcons he had handled longest. All he had to do was whistle once, and Lilah – that was the name the Prince had given the newcomer – flew to him. Two whistles and the eagle soared upwards, in search of prey.

Within a week of Lilah's arrival, Kasim discovered that, unlike the other birds, this one was able to play with him. He stuck a grape between his teeth. Lilah plucked adroitly and gobbled it down. The Prince offered her more grapes and then peaches and figs. And as the bird ate, it squawked happily, nibbling at the Princes's ears and ruffling his hair while he stroked her feathers as tenderly as he would a woman's hair.

One day the Prince's grandmother Sara, a gypsy of African descent, saw Kasim caressing the golden bird. The two of them were playing in the garden and as usual the Prince was feeding Lilah figs and peaches. She refused to eat the mice the other birds ate. As she watched them, Sara's nutmeg skin grew as pale as a peeled almond. Her body began quivering as she felt herself drawn into a world where the future is clear as daylight.

'Kasim,' said Sara, half in a daze. 'That bird of yours has magical powers and will help you find a wife. Be careful of her. She is not what she seems.'

Much though he loved his grandmother, Kasim laughed: 'Of course she's special, Nana. Lilah's a beauty. But, I've got a matchmaker already! I don't need another one with *you* around.'

'You think I'm an old fool, Kasim, don't you? Mark my words,' Sara insisted, 'this bird is going to tear open your heart and make you anew.'

The next evening, as the Prince was taking a stroll through the palace grounds in the moonlight, he came across a woman embroidering a wedding shawl. The woman's skin was pale, her eyes piercing but gentle, and her hair fell down her back with the abundance of the Al-Andalus sun in summer. Kasim loved her the moment he saw her.

'Shouldn't you be sewing inside?' he asked, anxious in case the stranger strained her eyes, or any harm came to her while sitting alone in the gardens.

'I'm happy where I am,' the woman replied.

'May I keep you company?'

The woman nodded and returned to her sewing.

'Who are you? I haven't seen you here before,' said Kasim.

The woman looked up, put a finger on her lips and remained silent. The Prince, content to be quiet, stayed by the woman's side until just before dawn, when she got up and disappeared into the palace gardens.

Every night after that Kasim went for a walk in the gardens of the Alcázar. And every night he sat beside the woman beneath a bower of trailing jasmine. He watched her silently, breathing in her beauty with the scent of flowers as she toiled on the wedding shawl. Night after night he observed the mysterious stranger and courted her with gifts of candied ginger, sugared almonds and the finest silk thread to use in embroidering the shawl.

At last, unable to contain his curiosity a moment longer, Kasim asked, 'Is that wedding shawl that you're making for you?'

The woman shook her head sadly. 'I shall never marry again,' she confessed. And then taking pity on him and the unasked questions she saw in the Prince's eyes, she went on to explain herself.

'My name is Romilly,' she said. 'I come from the Orkney Islands of the Norselands. I used to be married to Cullen the Carouser, King of Orkney, but when I couldn't give him the son he wanted, I ran away because he no longer loved me.'

'Where do you live in Seville?' Kasim asked. 'Tell me, so I can come and visit you tomorrow morning.'

The woman smiled, then changed the subject by saying: 'I'm embroidering this wedding shawl for the four daughters I left behind.' She lifted up the shawl and the Prince saw that it was covered with birds. 'This dove is my last born, Jewel. I see with my woman's eye that she has already chosen a man and wants to marry him. The peacock here, with its green and turquoise feathers, is my daughter Jezebel. She has crossed the sea with her Prince, while Delilah, my second child, is this kingfisher. I see her living in the Orient in a palace of marble and mother-of-pearl. It is my third child I worry about, Kasim. Her name is Jael. Her independent spirit prevents her choosing a husband.' Romilly sighed, then clasped the Prince's hands, a plea for sympathy in her eyes: 'I'm here to fetch her heart's desire: a man her equal who will love her well. For only when I've embroidered this last bird and my daughters are settled, will I be free of my past.'

The Prince noticed that the last bird on the shawl was a raven with one of its wings stitched in purple silk. The rest was unfinished.

Before dawn, at her usual hour, Romilly left the Prince. This time, however, instead of returning to his rooms in the Alcázar, he followed her.

He crept behind her as she slipped between tropical palms. Stepping over rambling roses, Romilly wove in and out of the yucca plants that grew in the palace gardens. The Prince watched her hide the wedding shawl under a bush. Then just as dawn was about to break, she opened the aviary door and stepped inside. To Kasim's amazement, the moment the first rays of sunlight touched Romilly's pale skin, she became Lilah – the golden eagle.

For three days and three nights Kasim stayed in his rooms, too frightened to come out. How could he have been so unlucky? How could he have fallen in love with a creature who was a woman at night and a bird by day? Kasim walked up and down the marble floor of his chamber, cursing his misfortune at finding the eagle.

'Sara was right,' he said out loud. 'That old witch, my grandmother, was right after all. That bird is more extraordinary than I could ever have imagined. Why, of all the women in the world, have I fallen in love with a bird-woman?' Eventually the Prince sat down exhausted. There was only one thing to do: he would go and see his grandmother and ask her advice.

When Kasim found her, the old woman was on the patio, arranging carnations in a turquoise vase.

'Aha,' she smiled, seeing the Prince's ashen face. 'So you've finally discovered the eagle's secret. Like I told you, she has magical powers. Doesn't she?'

Kasim nodded, letting out a heartbroken sob.

'Don't be sad my dear boy,' said Sara. 'You should be pleased for yourself. That bird is going to find you an excellent wife, a woman without equal, Kasim.'

'Don't you understand? I don't want anybody else, Nana. I love *her*! I want to marry Romilly.'

'That's what you think at the moment but the truth is that she doesn't want to marry *you*. You're going to have to learn patience, my boy. Just wait till you see the woman the bird is going to choose for you. When you see her, you'll discover what true love really is.'

That night Prince Kasim left his rooms to walk in the palace gardens once again. He found Romilly sitting beneath an orange tree, the wedding shawl spread over her lap. When she heard the familiar sound of the Prince's step she looked up, her face paler than a winter moon.

'So you know what I am,' she said, 'and why I have come to you. Don't be frightened Kasim. I will protect you and your children's children. Together we will travel in search of your bride. By the time we find her, I'll have finished this wedding shawl and you will set me free.'

***

At the end of the week, the falconer Prince set off on his journey to find a wife with the magic eagle perched on his wrist. They travelled through the land of the Gauls and over the mountains and valleys of the Norselands, testing hundreds of Princesses to see if one of them was suitable. But whenever Kasim asked Lilah to sit on a Princess's arm, the poor woman either ran away screaming or the eagle's talons dug so deep that she howled in pain.

At last the travellers arrived on the island of Rousay. Romilly, a woman by night in the Prince's tent, was putting the finishing touches to the wedding shawl.

'I can see with my woman's eye,' she told Kasim, 'that my daughter's heart has softened and she's ready to marry now. All that remains is for the right man to appear. There, the final stitch is in place.'

Lifting up the shawl, Romilly spread it over the cushions in the tent. The raven was finally complete, its fierce eyes glittering as its feathers shone in purple and black silk.

'Give this to my daughter if she agrees to marry you,' she said, handing the shawl to the Prince. Then, sensing an air of dejection hovering over Kasim, she tried to ease the pain of their parting with a final gift – an amulet that contained three of her golden feathers.

'Remember me with this,' Romilly said. 'Tell your youngest son to pass it down from one generation to the next, always leaving it in the care of his youngest child. If any of your descendants need my protection, all they have to do is break the amulet and call me.'

Kasim accepted the gift and thanked the bird-woman warmly.

The next day, after explaining the purpose of his visit to the King of Orkney, who was delighted by the opportunity to marry off his stubborn daughter, the Prince was formally introduced to Jael.

She looked the Prince up and down, found him pleasant and so agreed to submit herself to the test. If you were to ask Jael why she did so, she would say that there was something about the eagle's eyes which r e m i n d - ed her of the past. Of course, when the bird land- ed effortless- ly on Jael's arm without

leaving the slightest blemish, there was great ju-
bilation on the islands of Orkney.

Enchanted by the Princess, as she was with him,
Kasim handed her the magnificent wedding shawl
of birds.

'How strange,' Jael murmured. 'Everything about
you, Kasim, even this shawl, reminds me of my
mother. She used to embroider birds like this.
Perhaps she is still with us.'

Some say that Cullen the Carouser, the King of
Orkney wept bitter tears when he saw the wedding
shawl on his favourite daughter. It's hard to tell because by then he was an old man, and the eyes of
the old often weep. But when the shawl touched
Jael's shoulder, the golden eagle ascended into the
heavens and, swooping and diving, flew beyond the
clouds to kiss the sun.

5

The Fish-man of the Purple Lake

This is the story of the Fish-man who guards the Purple Lake at the bottom of the sea. They say the Fish-man was not always a monstrous creature with the legs and arms of a man and the head of a fish, but was once a beautiful boy called Musa from a region now known as Senegal. Musa came from the savannah lands of West Africa, where tall grasses blow in a landscape dotted with baobab trees.

Musa's parents scraped a living by growing millet and rice on a patch of land. His mother and father worked hard to raise their seven children: they laboured on the fields of their rich neighbours, sold drinking water to passing travellers, and the children, doing their part, gathered firewood to sell at the market every day.

Harvest after harvest, the family lived happily without much fat on their bones – until one year the rains failed. Across the savannah, grass shrivelled yellow, scorched dry by the sun. A coat of red dust settled on everything. The drought became so severe that wild animals forgot their differences and gathered around waterholes to wet their lips. When the animals began to migrate in search of water, Musa's father and mother began to plan how best to survive.

First, they sold their most prized possession: a goat whose milk the children drank once a week. Then, Musa's mother exchanged the gold earrings she wore at harvest celebrations for a sack of grain. When the grain was finished, Musa's father sold his favourite smock, embroidered in silver and gold thread, which he wore at weddings.

In the end there was nothing left to sell, and all the while little Musa, unaware that disaster crouched close by waiting to pounce on his family, played with his friends.

'We have to take Musa to a home where he will be fed properly,' said his father, watching the six-year-old kicking a ball made of leaves and animal hide. 'Even though hunger hasn't gnawed at his bones yet, our son will feel it soon if he remains with us.'

Musa's mother remained silent, afraid that if she spoke too soon, her emotions would betray her. Then, taking a deep breath, she said, 'Perhaps your uncle, the storyteller, will take him. I understand he is rich but kind. And since all his children are grown-up now, he may enjoy having a small boy at his side again.'

Her husband agreed.

Before Musa left home, his mother cradled him in her arms the way she used to when he was still a baby. The next morning when he awoke, she bathed her youngest son – rubbing oil on his skin till he gleamed, a black scorpion glinting in sunlight.

'Goodbye my son,' she said, after feeding Musa his favourite breakfast of millet porridge. 'You're

going far away today, but I shall always remain
close to you. Do you understand?'

Musa nodded. He couldn't really make sense of
what his mother was saying, but he could see from
the glitter of tears in her eyes that she was sad.

'I shall remain close to you, Musa,' his mother repeated. 'So close, in fact, that every now and again
I shall visit you in your dreams.'

The woman watched Musa leave the compound,
his head erect, walking beside his father. When
she lost sight of him, the tears she had been holding back began to fall.

Father and son walked for miles across the savannah lands until the farmer took to carrying Musa
on his shoulders. Occasionally they heard the cawing of geese flying north and saw antelopes leaping
across the horizon. The child, thrilled to be away
from home, looked gleefully at everything around
him. He heard baboons screeching in alarm as savannah hawks slowly circled the sky.

Three days later, the travellers approached the
village where Musa's rich great-uncle, the storyteller, lived with his wives and children.

'Before I take you into my uncle's compound, there
is something I want to give you,' the farmer said to
Musa. 'Just like you and my father before me, I am
the youngest son in my family. There is a tradition
in our family,' he said, removing a red amulet from

his pocket, 'that this should be given to the youngest boy in our line when he leaves home. It's yours Musa. Look after it carefully because it has magic properties.'

The farmer tied the amulet firmly around his son's neck and then told the story behind it. 'It's said that our ancestors were Moors, my son, a people who travelled south in search of farmland. Before we came here, we conquered a land across the sea. One of our line found his wife with the help of a woman who was a bird by day and took human form at night. The amulet around your neck contains her feathers. They will bring you good luck, Musa. Guard the amulet carefully and always remember who you are: a precious child of the soil, the son of an honourable but humble farmer.'

It was hard to tell how much Musa understood of what his father was saying to him. After all, he was only six years old and, though he was clever and hoped never to bring shame to his family, he was still a child. But as he waved his father goodbye his hand held the amulet, and he believed he would hold fast to his father's words: he was his father's son, a precious child of the soil.

***

A few days after Musa's arrival at his great-uncle's compound, the rains came – falling in fat drops like eggs smashing on the ground. The flamboyant trees flowered in showers of scarlet, and the sweet smell of frangipani wafted from inside the old man's compound throughout the village. Musa had never seen such abundance in his life. His great-uncle's granaries were loaded with sacks of corn, millet and rice, and each of his three wives cooked meat every day.

Everyone was kind to Musa, admiring his intelligence and commenting on the beauty of his appearance. 'Look how bright his blue-black eyes are,' women whispered. 'And look how straight and strong his limbs are growing,' said passers-by as they watched Musa running through the village.

The boy enjoyed living in his great-uncle's compound. He looked after the goats and ran errands for his aunts. For the most part, he was pleased with his new life. But sometimes at night, when mosquitoes disturbed his sleep and tree frogs croaked noisily, Musa remembered the family he had left behind and cried himself to sleep. Whenever this happened, his mother appeared in his dreams, singing the lullabies she'd once sung him when he was a baby.

On the second anniversary of his arrival at his great-uncle's house, the old man summoned Musa to sit beside him at the entrance to his room. 'I've been watching you,' the old man said, gazing at Musa through milky eyes. 'And I like your ways. You're modest and truthful, a credit to the family. I'd like to help you, but as you know I've already allocated my land to my sons. My only regret is that I have no one to teach the art of storytelling to. Would you like to learn, Musa?'

'But I am a child of the soil,' the boy replied, 'the son of a humble farmer.'

'Just like I was when I started out. It's often people like us who tell the best stories. Would you like to learn how to tell a story?'

Musa said that he would.

Every day after that, when he had finished herding goats and running errands, and had swept the compound clean, Musa joined the old man for lessons in storytelling. To begin with, he was given a kora to play – a large gourd of an instrument with many strings. His fingers learned how to pluck chords, nimbly stretching to make the sound of running water. Musa learned how to beat the side of the kora in imitation of armies marching to war.

Through listening to the old man's words, Musa learned to sing refrains within stories; to sing and play like a young woman smiling, a lioness prowling or a young man hunting.

'You're an excellent student,' said the old man. 'I believe that in time you'll become a master kora player and people will come to you to learn.'

Soon Musa became so adept with the instrument that his great-uncle asked him to accompany him when he performed at weddings. While the old man told stories that made the gathering laugh and then cry, Musa, dressed in fine embroidered clothes, sang melodious refrains. Strumming and plucking, he gently teased music from the gourd; music so moving that when the wedding guests heard it, they showered money over Musa.

One day, late in the afternoon, the old man summoned his great-nephew to sit down beside him. 'It is time you learned our stories,' he declared. 'It's time you moved on from simply singing my refrains.'

Musa was delighted. Hour after hour he sat with his great-uncle learning the stories of West African peoples. He laughed at the antics of Ananse the spider-man, folk hero of the Ashanti. He memorised the tales of travelling Fulani herdsmen, the stories of Wolof and Mandinka warriors and, finally, the adventures of magic hunters from Guinea, who fly by night and converse with spirits in daylight. Musa had never been happier in his life.

If his favourite Aunt happened to ask him for a story, he would pluck it like a feather from the amulet around his neck, and then grooming it with words, fluff it out, until the feather grew into a mighty pair of wings that flew to the listener like a golden bird. Every night, hugging the amulet, Musa recited the story that his great-uncle had taught him that day, repeating it till the rhythm of his words was exactly like that of the old man.

Musa became so enchanted by the stories he was learning that as he slept he dreamed he was a magic hunter, a victorious warrior. He was Musa, the son of a magnificent, powerful King; Musa, a great hero.

You wouldn't have noticed watching him grow into a young man that there was anything amiss in his character. At sixteen, Musa was given some of the old man's cattle to look after. He found them grazing-land, where the grass was moist with dew. Yet when he returned home from the savannah, there seemed less of the old Musa about him, and more of something new.

'He's becoming a man,' thought his favourite Aunt, as she handed him a bowl of cassava and guinea fowl. 'He keeps more of his heart to himself now.'

No one seemed to realise that Musa's love of stories was changing him. Alone with the cattle on the grasslands, he became the heroes he sang about. He was a warrior with a burning sword, a hunter with a spear that killed lions. He fought with the greatest of men, outwitting them. Then, after he'd forced them to bow down before him, men and women, old and young, threw garlands at his feet.

No one seemed to realise, when he sang at weddings, that the gleam of conviction in Musa's eyes was a sign that a craving for greatness was gnawing at his bones. 'Who respects a man who sweeps the yard like a woman and leads a handful of cattle to graze?' he asked himself. 'Or for that matter, who respects the son of a farmer, when those who are remembered are men who've performed extraordinary deeds? More than anything in the world I want to be a warrior!'

Before long, there wasn't a task he did in the old man's compound that pleased him. Whether he was feeding husks to goats or leading cattle to graze, he felt ashamed, believing that such chores were beneath him. Eventually, the old man, sensing the unease within Musa, called him to his side.

'Musa,' he said gently, 'you haven't been yourself for some time. Now that you're old enough to travel on your own, I think you should visit your family.'

Musa nodded, excited at the old man's suggestion. The old man gave Musa a gold necklace to take as a gift to his mother and a magnificent smock in blue, red and green to give to his father. 'Walk carefully on your journey home,' he said, after giving Musa his blessing. 'And when your visit is over and you're yourself again, you're very welcome to return to my house.'

***

The next day Musa set off on his journey. But instead of taking the path that would lead him back to his father's village, he walked due south to seek advice from Nana – a wise woman who lived deep in the forest and understood the wishes of the gods.

When he arrived at the forest's edge, Musa, pretending that his steel cutlass was a silver sword, slashed the undergrowth, notching a mark on the trees so he would be able to find his way out again. Cutting away creepers, he plunged deeper and deeper into the jungle, little knowing that a thousand hidden eyes were spying on him, warning Nana of his progress.

On the third day of his journey, Musa stumbled into a clearing where a thatched hut stood beside a crooked Nim tree. Sitting in the shade of the tree was a wizened woman, her grey hair plaited. She was throwing cowry shells to look into the future, and as the shells fell, she sang a rhyme to herself:

'Birds fly and spiders creep,
Men sometimes cry
But Musa shall weep.'

The old woman looked up and smiled. 'Musa,' she said, 'I was expecting you over an hour ago. What can I do for you?'

Without further ado, Musa sat down beneath the Nim tree and opened up his heart. 'I want to be famous,' he said. 'I want my dreams of glory to come true. Tell me, Nana, how can I make that happen? How can I make my name known?'

'Are you sure that's what you really want?'

'Oh yes,' Musa sighed.

Nana asked him to throw the cowry shells. He shook them in both his hands, blew his breath over them for good luck, and then flung them to the ground.

Nana shook her head sadly, for spread out before her like fragments of speckled eggshells was Musa's future. 'You have a gift for storytelling Musa, be satisfied,' she urged. 'Soon your fame will spread, and you will become a master kora player and a great storyteller. Go home, Musa.'

'But I want to be a great hunter and warrior,' the young man replied.

Nana asked him to throw the cowry shells a second time and once again she told him to go home and be satisfied with his lot.

'Why won't you help me?' Musa cried. 'I know I'm the son of a humble farmer, but that shouldn't stop you from telling me how I can become a magnificent warrior so that I too will be someone people sing about.'

'So you won't heed my warning? Didn't you hear my song, Musa?'

The old woman repeated the rhyme, but this time she sang slowly so that every word of the song could be heard:

'Birds fly and spiders creep,

Men sometimes cry,
But Musa shall weep.'

'Don't you know it's dangerous to tamper with your destiny?' she said. 'Put aside your childish dreams. Go home a man, my son!'

Having travelled so deeply into the forest, Musa couldn't turn his back on his dreams. So at last, realising that nothing she said would dissuade him, Nana asked him to throw the shells a third time.

After carefully weighing up what the cowries were telling her, Nana said: 'In the savannah lands near your home, Musa, lives a magic elephant, who many warriors have tried to destroy. This elephant has a name: Imoro. He's as black as ebony and as strong as twenty hippopotamuses. His only weakness is that he can't resist wild honey. If you succeed in killing him, Musa, you must grind his tusks to powder and then drink them with milk. Then you'll have all the power you need to perform extraordinary deeds. But be careful,' Nana added. 'Hold your amulet close when you're near Imoro, for should you fail in your task your fate will be fearful indeed.'

Musa thanked the old woman for her advice and following the trail he'd made, found his way out of the forest. A week later, he reached a town near the village where his parents lived and headed for the market. He looked around until he found what he was searching for: a table laden with jars of wild honey.

'Come and buy, come and buy,' a woman sitting at the stall yelled as she suckled her baby.

'Will you give me all the honey that you have in exchange for this trinket?' Musa asked. He opened the package that his great-uncle had asked him to give to his mother.

The trader's eyes widened at the sight of such a chunky gold necklace.

'I want every single jar of your honey,' Musa explained, 'and a cart and ox to pull it.'

The woman stared at Musa, shifting her baby from one breast to the other. 'Aren't you the child of Musa Baba?' she asked, mentioning the name of Musa's father. 'Aren't you the child he sent away during the great drought?'

'Indeed I'm not,' Musa replied.

'Are you sure? Your face looks just like Musa Baba's when he was younger, and your hands remind me of his before they grew rough tilling soil.'

'I assure you, I don't know who you're talking about,' said Musa. 'Will you or won't you sell me your honey?'

'Of course,' the woman said, quickly pocketing the necklace. She then called a boy to her side who arranged for all the honey to be placed on an ox-drawn cart.

Musa left the market, pulling the ox and cart behind him. After a couple of miles, he stopped at the roadside to drink cold water from a calabash. As he quenched his thirst, he heard the plaintive cry of an old man singing to a kora. Musa followed the sound till he found its source. The man, sitting beneath a flowering frangipani, was playing a silver-studded kora, the most beautiful instrument Musa had ever seen.

'Will you give me your kora in exchange for this outfit?' Musa asked, unpacking the hand-woven smock in blue, red and green that his great-uncle had asked him to give to his father.

The old man studied Musa's face carefully. 'Aren't you the son of Musa and Meta Baba, who was sent away and is now a kora player?' he enquired, naming Musa's parents. 'Your face is like his and so is your voice. In fact, when I saw you walking towards me, I thought Musa Baba had become young once again.'

'I don't know who you're talking about,' Musa said. 'Will you or won't you sell me your kora?'

'I can hardly refuse,' replied the old man. 'Age has cracked my voice, and I shall soon need a fine smock to wear with my shroud. You may take this kora with pleasure.'

Satisfied with his purchases, Musa began the long journey deep into the savannah lands, to perform the deed that would make him famous; the deed that would make him the greatest warrior of all time.

There are places in West Africa where few men have walked, which echo with the hum of another world. Places where the songs of birds and the cries of animals sound strange because they are swept along by a cold, dry wind that blows from the Sahara. In one such space the grass, rustling uneasily, listens to the tread of a new step. It is Musa, silver kora slung over his shoulder, pulling the ox-cart of wild honey. Musa is tired and thirsty and glistens with sweat.

Unloading his cargo, he ties the ox to a tree and begins digging a hole. He lines the cavity with smooth, flat stones and when he has finished, pours in jar after jar of wild honey.

'What is this man doing and what is his mission here?' ask invisible spectators behind twitching grasses. They have never seen this before, a man emptying honey into a deep hole.

Soon, ants, smelling the sweet scent, cluster around the rim; with them come hornets and flies. Musa sits beneath the tree and begins singing to his kora. His voice cuts through the air with chords that drive the insects away.

The wind carries Musa's message to birds, who sing it to every animal in the savannah. Lions, leopards and antelopes hear the song. They pass the

message on to crocodiles and buffalo, till eventually
it reaches the animal for which it is intended: the
black elephant, Imoro, wallowing in a pool of water.

'Your friend Musa invites you to a feast of wild
honey,' the animals cry. 'He is sitting beside a tree
waiting for you. Come quickly, Imoro, for the honey is good.'

Imoro, resplendent in his black skin, his white
tusks gleaming in the sun, slowly rises from the
pool. He steps out, following a bird who takes him
to Musa.

The young man singing with the voice of a friend
invites Imoro, the magic elephant, to eat. At first
the animal is suspicious. Men have tried to trick
him before but no one has ever presented him
with his favourite food of wild honey. Imoro sniffs
Musa's scent and steps back. He sniffs again. What
he senses confirms what he hears: the soothing
balm of a young man's music.

Imoro steps forward licking the basin of honey
from the rim to the centre. Very soon all the honey
is eaten and, kneeling down in gratitude, he wraps
his trunk around Musa's neck and caresses him.

At once, the young man's voice becomes like that
of a mother singing her child to sleep – the kora,
a fountain trickling in the background. And while
Imoro nuzzles Musa's neck, stroking the red amulet, the young man is thinking, 'First I must kill

him. Then I must cut off his tusks, grind them to powder and drink them with milk, so that at last I will be the greatest of all warriors.'

Imoro's eyes are closing. He is almost asleep. He dozes as Musa prepares to strike.

***

Musa set the kora aside and slowly inched his hand behind his back to where he had hidden a cutlass. Imoro's eyes flickered open and then shut again, the way eyes often do when closing in sleep. Musa raised his arm, the cutlass glinting.

Just at the moment he was about to slam the weapon on Imoro's head, the elephant opened its eyes again. The trunk, caressing Musa's neck, jerked and as it did so, the amulet around Musa's neck tore open, tumbling to the ground.

The cutlass came crashing down but instead of wounding Imoro, it tore a gaping hole in the earth. Realising that he had been tricked, Imoro shrieked with rage. He shrieked a second time, his tusks poised, his trunk about to dash Musa to the ground.

'Magic amulet,' the young man cried, petrified. 'Help me! Magic bird who helped my ancestor, please come to my aid. Imoro, the magic elephant, is about to kill me!'

Three golden feathers from the amulet fluttered into life, and all at once became a gigantic golden eagle. Musa didn't know which to be more frightened of: the shining bird or the black elephant. Both were enormous and both stood, side by side, glaring at him.

It was the eagle who spoke first and in the voice of the Orcadian Queen, Romilly. 'Musa,' she said, 'you've brought shame to the family I've protected for years. I never imagined when I befriended your ancestor that one day I would be called to defend a man who dared forsake his family. What vain dreams of glory have possessed you, Musa? What foolish fantasies have led you to this?'

Musa trembled before the eagle and the elephant, and for the first time in years he longed to feel the touch of his mother's hand and hear the voice of his father speaking. Even though he had pretended not to know them, Musa would have gladly exchanged his dreams of glory to be back in his family compound again.

'I'd like to crush you to death,' trumpeted Imoro, 'but the eagle here says she has a better punishment in mind for you.'

'Indeed,' said the bird. 'You wanted to be a warrior Musa, and now you will become one. Hidden in the Indian Ocean at the bottom of a mountain range is the Purple Lake. Your task will be to guard the lake with a sword made of a thousand shark's teeth. You will stay there, alone and underwater, until the gods finally take pity on you.'

Grabbing hold of him by the wrists, the golden eagle carried Musa across the African continent, casting a dark shadow as she flew over the desert. When she reached an expanse of water, she circled until her eagle eyes saw the Purple Lake below. Then, from hundreds of feet up in the sky, she cast Musa into the sea.

Musa turned and twisted, somersaulting, convinced that his life was over. He turned and, as he flipped over a third time, he dropped the red amulet. He tumbled through dark clouds, hurtling down to the sea. As soon as he touched the water, he turned into the Fish-man: a monstrous creature with human arms and legs, and the body and head of a fish.

Musa languished in his watery prison beside the Purple Lake. He was grateful, to begin with, that his life had been spared. But as the lake snarled and snapped at him like a bad tempered dog, he grew lonely and yearned for friendship. And yet if anything – be it a smiling dolphin, a porpoise, or a laughing clownfish – came close to the lake, Musa's friendly nature became possessed by a warrior spirit and he became the Fish-man. And then, waving the sword of shark's teeth, he chased everything away; even though deep in his heart what he wanted most in the world was a friend.

Day after day he wept into the lake, which spat back at him angrily. 'If only I had known how hollow the life of a warrior can be,' he cried. 'If I had known, I would have been content as a storyteller. No one told me it would be so lonely fighting everything in sight.'

What's more, remembering his love for the kora, Musa tried to make one out of reeds and conch shells. But his hands, hardened by wielding the sword, broke the strings and he wept more bitterly.

At last the day came when Ajuba, the fisherman's daughter, swam over the lake with her friend, Whale. She dropped a whale's carbuncle into the Purple Lake to find the path to where her father lay buried by the sea.

A hissing serpent sprang from the lake. Musa, who was fast asleep, was woken up by the serpent's voice. Ajuba was the first human he had seen during his life as the Fish-man. He wanted to talk to her. He wanted to hear the latest news of the land of men. But just as soon as this desire for friendship welled up within him, the warrior spirit possessed him again and, wielding the sword of a thousand shark's teeth, he chased Ajuba and Whale away.

Musa returned to the lake crying. He was so distressed that he lifted his sword over his head and threw it into the Purple Lake. Then he knelt down, begging the gods to take pity on him. The hissing serpent reared up again, swaying from side to side.

'Go home, Musa,' she said. 'You have served your time. Go back home.'

'But how can I return?' he asked.

'Swim to the surface. The Bird-woman is waiting up there to take you home again.'

Musa did as he was told. The moment he breathed air again, his true nature returned to him and his fish-body fell away. He was Musa, a handsome young man once again, and circling above him was Romilly the golden eagle. She hauled Musa up in to the sky and then carried him back to his father's village.

No one could believe their eyes when they saw Musa walking through the compound gates. They had given him up for dead. Musa's mother threw her arms around him, delighted he was home again. And his father, now a very old man, ordered a cow to be killed in thanks for his son's return.

The family celebrated for three days and on the fourth day Musa's great-uncle arrived, laden with gifts. He brought cattle and goats and fabulous cloths for Musa's mother and father. Most important of all, he gave the young man a new kora so that he could return to storytelling.

Musa lived to be an old man and, just as Nana had foretold with the cowry shells, he became a famous storyteller and a master kora player. One of his most popular stories is the tale of the Fish-man, which he claims is a true story. No one believes him, except for his wife Binta. Only she knows that whenever Musa washes in the sea, tiny silver fish scales appear on his back. Thankfully, they live a long way from the sea.

Acknowledgements

My thanks go to my grandmother, Mame Soma, whose skill as a storyteller instilled in me a love of her craft. My thanks also to Julie and Norman Gibson, who introduced me to the beautiful islands of Orkney, and Helen Hake, the first reader of *The Fisherman's Daughter*. Finally, a huge thank you to Bibi Bakare-Yusuf of Cassava Republic, whose perseverance and commitment brought this collection of stories to life.